Little
Bandaged
Days.

Little Bandaged Days.

Kyra Wilder

PICADOR

First published 2020 by Picador
an imprint of Pan Macmillan
The Smithson, 6 Briset Street, London EC1M 5NR
Associated companies throughout the world
www.panmacmillan.com

ISBN 978-1-5290-1737-3

1 3 5 7 9 8 6 4 2

A CIP catalogue record for this book is available from the British Library.

Typeset by Palimpsest Book Production Ltd, Falkirk, Stirlingshire

Printed and bound by CPI Group (UK) Ltd, Croydon, CR0 4YY

Visit **www.picador.com** to read more about all our books
and to buy them. You will also find features, author interviews and
news of any author events, and you can sign up for e-newsletters
so that you're always first to hear about our new releases.

For Alan,

and for Dashiell,
and for Dexter,
and for Daley

It's harder to burn down a house than you think.

Shirley Jackson

Part One

1

It wasn't true, what my mother said, when I called to show her the apartment, about the light. I held the phone up and tiptoed around while E and B napped but she only kept saying, It's so dark! I can't see a thing! You always live in the darkest places! Isn't there a window you can open? she said. I'm worried about you!

I told her I was fine, that it was amazing here. That E had fed swans by the lake. That I had already learned to say bonjour. Bonjour, I said, and wiggled my fingers at her through the screen. I wanted her to see me like that, speaking French I mean. I had a baguette in the kitchen for her to see too, lying half cut on the wooden board with some piece or other of cheese next to it. A cherry tomato. She said she couldn't see inside the kitchen.

Turn on a light. Ohforgoodnesssake, she said. The signal wasn't really very good in the apartment so her words came

3

out all at once or not at all and her face either jerked around the screen or was frozen.

Ohforgoodnesssake, she said again. I wiggled my fingers at the screen in a goodbye sort of way and mouthed, I LOVE YOU, slow, like I was shouting it.

Talk soon, I said, hoping she could hear me and air-smooched and pushed the red button to send her away.

Ohforgoodnesssake. She would have said that again, she would have been unhappy when I hung up on her like that, she wouldn't have liked it a bit, but E would be up soon and I wanted to have a snack ready for her.

I liked the light, the half-light really, in the apartment. It was grey, soothing. To me it felt like the inside of an oyster. Delicate and safe and tucked away with us inside it. Everything was cool and clean and new.

The ceilings were low. That was true. My mother had been right about that. Well what did I expect? The apartment was on the ground floor of a hulking great concrete building. A dumpy grey block that made no concessions to those that might be looking at it. It didn't bow, or straighten up, or take off its hat. It only squatted on its patch of gravel, like a dog maybe, shitting in the grass.

I loved that about it. I specifically did, especially when I tumbled out of it in the morning with B, with E, with my hair a bit more wild than I would have liked and my skirt not matching my shirt, and everything pilled and wrinkled and pulling at me. I liked to have it behind me, my great big ugly building with my beautiful apartment nestled safe inside it like a pearl.

It didn't even have balconies or window boxes, the building. It wasn't that kind of place. If the people that lived in the other apartments had beautiful things, if they were stylish, if they loved flowers, lace underwear or a particular shade of purple, they kept all this to themselves, behind their various doors. I had heard that was the way of things here, and it seemed to be true. People kept to themselves. Only, if you were out walking and threw something into the bin and missed and pretended not to, or really didn't, see that you'd missed and started to walk away from the wrapper or receipt that was lying next to, but not in, the bin, then people would talk to you. Did you see that? they would say. Did you see what you just did?

There was a park with a sandbox and a water pump behind the building. We could get there by means of a little path that led between our building and the identical one next to it. I liked the path because it was always filled with tiny old ladies walking tiny old dogs and I could practise saying bonjour to them and they would nod and smile no matter how garbled I sounded. Sometimes speaking French was like having your mouth filled with rocks and expecting your tongue to just leap, flying over all the dips and drops and cracks in the words, in the sounds of them.

Our first Saturday in the apartment, M and I had made a great show of buying real Swiss-made toys to use at the park. E had chosen each toy with that grave attention particular to four-year-olds: an adjustable hand rake, a trowel and a miniature hoe. The tools were made out of wood and metal, painted red, and on each handle a tiny Swiss flag had been drawn by hand. B, being only a baby, didn't need a toy of course, but we bought him a wooden cow to set by his crib, to watch him sleep with its peaceful hand-painted eyes. They were expensive, the tools, the cow, but M laughed away the price at the register. We were going to live like real Swiss people: toys would be handmade, expensive, beautiful, sparse and practical. For the tools we also bought the matching red-leather carry bag. We kept them by the door and I loved holding them as much as E did. The soft weight of the perfectly turned wood felt pure and promising against my skin, as if in Switzerland the trees grew without splinters, and took the shape of handles easily, without even needing to be cut. Everything was right and natural and clean, everything fell into line and stayed there.

M and me, we did our best to fall in with everyone else, into the place that was natural for us. We took a tourist train up to the mountains and breathed in air that made us feel like we'd never been alive before right then. When we took the tools to the park we cleaned each one at the pump before we went home. We dusted and polished them, ferreting out every individual grain of sand, rubbing the red paint with the soft ends of our shirts until it shone.

It was true that the apartment was small. On that point too, Mother was right and there was no denying it. But, I told E, small is wonderful! When we are packed up tight inside it, I told her, the apartment is small like a treasure chest, and that means we turn into gems when we step inside. What are you today? I'd ask her, when we squeezed through the front door with our shopping, and she would always say a diamond and I would pick something different every time so she would learn the names of the different stones. Emeralds are green, Sapphires are blue, Rubies are red and I love you. See? We could make anything wonderful, anything fun.

A lady from the relocation agency provided by M's new office had shown us the apartment on a tour of possible living spaces. Pick one, the memo from M's office had read and so we did. All we had to do was put our finger on the one we wanted.

The lady had been sent to us by the agency because of her excellent English.

Oh my god! she said whenever we walked into a new room in one of the apartments on our tour. She liked also to raise a hand to her mouth.

I liked the way her heels clicked on the parquet floors when she walked into a room ahead of us, and the way she said, Zis way, and, Oh my god! as if she were still speaking French. But I didn't like the way she only asked me to open the drawers in the kitchens or to peek inside the washing machines to see how big they were. Zee? she would say, For you! And I supposed that really they were for me, weren't they? The kitchen drawers and the washing machines. Well, they certainly weren't for the lady from the agency in her jacket and pencil skirt and clicking shoes. My clothes and E's clothes and B's were the only clothes that could be crumpled up into a washing machine. M's clothes and her clothes, the clothes of working people, would of course have to be seen to at the dry cleaners. It seemed I hadn't realized this until we all stood together, M and me and her and E and B, in front of the washing machine in one of the apartments and she had said, ceremoniously, 'Ere, zis is for you. But of course I must have seen that from the beginning. What was for me I mean.

M had a whole new set of European suits for the office, Italian or English maybe. Fitted. Half-lined and light for summer. He looked really good. He had new sunglasses with little round lenses and tortoiseshell frames that he took on and off when we walked into apartments and out of them. His new leather loafers were so soft inside that I had actually gasped when I slipped them on, once, at the hotel, while he was asleep. I had actually gasped.

We chose the apartment closest to M's work. Besides, M said, it's only temporary, next year we'll buy a house on the lake. Won't you like that, he said. I liked the apartment though, I liked being close to him during the day. Me and the kids at home, him at work, all of us close. If E locks me in the bathroom, I could just yell and you could come get me out, I said to M.

Oh non, the lady from the agency interrupted. You must not yell here. In Switzerland we are quiet. We are always like mouzes in ze houzes. She said *the* like this, *ze*, and I really loved it. Like mouzes in ze houzes, I said quietly to myself. All right, I said, no yelling. The lady still looked at me though, cautiously, as if I might do anything, even though I said I wouldn't yell. In Switzerland we are quiet, she said again. Well.

There was a bedroom for M and me, a small room for the toilet and another for the shower and the washing machine. The kitchen was in a room all by itself with two doors that could be closed and locked, one leading to the living room and the other to the front entryway. There was even a tiny bedroom for E with a bed and a table and a desk. In E's room everything was touching everything else, the bed was touching the desk, the table was touching the bed. Everything was small and fine, and one day M brought home a quilt stitched all over with trailing crocuses and forget-me-nots and the room came alive around it and was perfect and fit E like a glove.

There was also a room with nothing in it that could be reached through a small door in the living room. It might have been a large closet or a small bedroom. The ceilings felt higher there, well, they were higher. Oh my god! the lady from the agency had said when we saw it. There was a plant in a pot, a succulent with stalks like the arms of an octopus, a small hand sink, and a scorch mark burned into the floor.

Oh my god! the lady from the agency said again, and put her hand almost up to her mouth but not quite touching it. Patting my arm, winking at my husband, she said, Somezing for you! A little place! Oh, yes, zis is tiptop!

I had met her once before, the lady from the agency, at her office, by her own request. Zo she could get to know me, she said, talking with M and me on speakerphone. Because we know who it will be picking ze apartment, she said. I could hear the wink in her voice and started to say, No, but M said, Yes! Of course! And so I dug the put-away, then packed-at-the-last-minute, navy blazer I used to wear to meetings out of my bag, brushed my hair, and went alone so she could get a look at me and decide on the kind of places she might offer up.

I had to wait to see her when I got there, she was a busy woman, but I was given a home-design magazine in English. I was also given a thimble of coffee in a tiny porcelain cup. There was a chocolate perched on the side of the saucer and I was pointed into a chair that seemed to take me in its polished arms and set me straight. The magazine, for some reason, featured a series of close-up photographs of people's feet on tiptoe, taken from behind. In all the photos the feet were poised directly above some delicate thing, their heels only just touching it. One heel hovered over an orange, another over a lime. There were several shots of heels with eggs underneath them. They were all curves and soft shadows, and I found my eyes drifting over them and thinking, in the quiet of the office, away from E, from B, where no one needed me right away, that it might be possible to prefer one sort of thing over another. Even small things, that it might be possible to consider: orange, or lime, or egg. It might be possible to think quietly of things like that, to make up my mind. The coffee was hot, and sweet in just the right way and I slipped the chocolate whole between my teeth.

Once we moved into the apartment, I kept the children out of the empty room. Perhaps it was for me: a little place. B slept in a small collapsible crib in the living room. Or that was the idea, for him to sleep there, but he was the sort of baby that preferred to cling to its mother at night and be walked and walked and walked and talked to. So mostly that's what we did, at night, walk in circles. Living room, entryway, kitchen, living room. Here we are, I whispered to him over and over and over again, my lips pressed against his snail-shell ear.

Sometimes, after he finally, finally, fell asleep I crept into the spare room and lay on the floor and called my mother. The signal ringing out of my midnight or one or two in the morning into her middle of the day. She was always eating lunch and would talk to me as she chewed and I would listen and sometimes fall asleep. The daylight always amazed me when she answered, even though it was only science, the most usual thing, to see her tiny and far away, wrapped in sunlight, blazing. There was always so much light, when I called her, there at the end of my wrist.

We had arrived in Switzerland pushing suitcases packed tight with the few things we'd decided to keep. The rest, the furniture, the silverware, the wedding plates with the bamboo pattern painted in seafoam green I'd spent such a long time picking out, had been given to friends or sold to strangers back home. Even B's crib. Even the rug beneath the crib.

Ohforgoodnesssake, my mother said, when she asked about one thing or another thing. The hand-caned chairs we'd had in the living room say, or my grandmother's creamer and sugar dish. Basically all of it was gone. How could we have kept it? We were disposing of things, cleaning up after ourselves. Don't you want to keep this? my mother asked me, walking around the house, our beautiful emptying, empty house. Or this? I wasn't listening to her though, I was already elsewhere, already on the plane, already in the new place.

M had been worried about taking the job. It was, after all, a difficult one. Many people would be working for him, depending on him, waiting to hear what he had to say. I'm not sure, he'd said, holding the contract. I remember him saying it. I remember him looking at the line that was waiting for his signature, how the terms and conditions swirled over the beautiful white paper like smoke.

I'd told him he should, that he could. I'll have to work longer, more hours, he said. I'll have to travel. I'll see you less. I'll see E and B less. Everything will be fine, I said, you work, and I'll take care of everything else. Everything will be so wonderful, you'll see. You can do this, I said, you should.

M had signed the contract, of course, and we were flown over and the moment we stumbled out of the airport he was snapped up because he was needed urgently already at work. I saw for one second before he got into the car that he was nervous. It was his face. I saw also that he was going to have to be someone else here, and from now on. Maybe neither one of us had seen that before then. A car had been waiting for him and he was sped away without us. There was another car for me and the kids and the bags. The driver was quite friendly and I hesitated the whole way about the tip and missed the places he was telling me about while I tried desperately to calculate appropriate amounts.

I always loved to travel but foreign countries have a way of making me doubt my instincts. In the end I didn't have any money, my wallet was in M's jacket pocket, so I had to smile terribly at the driver and sink lower and lower into the ground as he unloaded each one of our too heavy bags. He waited for a moment by his car, but I only smiled harder at him. I wanted him to understand that I was a good person. He left.

The hotel was a really nice one with views of the lake and the Jet d'Eau from the windows of our suite. Once we'd been helped into our room I found a cartoon on the TV for E and ordered a pot of coffee to be sent up even though it was the equivalent of thirty US dollars. I told the lady at reception to charge it to the room. It came on a silver tray complete with a pitcher of steamed milk and a warm cup. I sat on the toilet seat in the white marble bathroom and drank the whole thing while B dozed in front of the TV and E asked, What are they saying, what are they saying, what are they saying. Why are they saying those funny words, she asked. Why are they speaking that way?

It's French, I said. It's beautiful. Soon, I said, you'll sound like that too. She buttoned her lips at this, frowning. No, she said.

Oui, I said, and laughed.

We were only at the hotel for a week maybe, but the hours there passed like a dream, one opening easily onto the next, like an endless stream of French doors, all linen curtains, gentle breezes and light. M left the hotel early for work. Every morning he wore one of his new suits. B and E and I luxuriated in our jet lag. We slept when we wanted to and lingered late over the hotel breakfast. We spread berry jams from tiny jars onto thick slices of bread we cut ourselves from loaves the size of suckling pigs. Three-minute eggs came to the table with their own tiny spoons if we asked for them, their tops just waiting to be cracked. Pistachio nougat could be cut from a large block and brought to the table, likewise, if we asked for it, as could hot chocolate, as could bacon, as could pieces of honeycomb sliced from an actual hive.

We went out exploring. Exploring in a proprietary way I suppose, not like tourists. Well we weren't, tourists I mean. We were home. We crossed back and forth over the lake, traversing the jaunty zigzagging bridges. We walked by the jewellery stores that rose in a glaring white wall, springing right out of the glittering lake. Tiffany, Bulgari, Piaget, Harry Winston, Chopard, Graff. We peeked inside to look at the beautiful ladies who were selling, at the beautiful ladies who were buying.

E stared hard through a window at a little girl about her own age. The girl wore a pink fur vest over a belted dress. She sat very still in a tufted chair. She was watching a woman in a black tailored suit slip watches onto her mother's slim wrist. At least, I imagine the woman was her mother. They wore their hair in similar loose waves. A shop assistant offered the girl a chocolate but she shook her head. E watched this as if stunned.

We stopped at each display window to see the latest and the best. For you, E said to me, as we walked along, pointing at all the sparkling things. The necklaces that looked like chandeliers or snakes. The bangles and watches and rings. For you, for you, for you, she said and I smiled at her my biggest and my best smile, the one that told her, I am so happy, don't you see how happy I am. You have a happy, happy mother, my smile said. We are a happy family in a beautiful place. I pushed B along in his stroller with one hand and said to her, Thank you, I love you, thank you, I love you, thank you, I love you.

We walked along the backstreets too. Twisting, when the mood struck us, further into wherever we happened to be. We wandered past little run-down cigarette kiosks and underneath scruffy buildings shuttered in yellow and green. Walking behind the Parc Bertrand I looked up and saw an old woman on a mouldering balcony watering her geraniums topless. Her magnificently sagging breasts brushed the tops of her pink and red blossoms, deadheading them maybe.

Once, we walked all the way to the Bois de la Bâtie and stood on the small pedestrian bridge over the point where the two rivers, the Rhône and the Arve, met. Look, I said to E, pointing, making sure she noticed that the rivers were two different colours. Making sure she saw the way they swirled together, the way they stayed apart. Afterwards, we walked up the hill to the library and found books about rivers written in beautiful inscrutable French. Well, we were here, in a way, to be lost, to lose ourselves. Why else would we have come?

I loved it in the hotel. I loved the days. I called my mother many times and told her this. I told her that everything was new and everything was wonderful. White buildings, red-tiled roofs, blue lake, jewels and chocolate everywhere you looked. Fresh. It was June, and the rain kept away. The sun never got too hot. There was always a cool breeze coming off the lake.

If I wanted to take E to the lake to feed the swans, the lady at the reception desk would give us bags of stale bread, and while we were gone maids would go into our room and make the beds for us. I told M he could leave us in the hotel for ever. I told him he could leave me anywhere where there were plenty of young men with silver trays of coffee who would come to my room whenever I rang for them. He laughed and said, Sure, stay for ever, but of course then the memo appeared and we had to find an apartment.

The last night in the hotel I put E and B to bed early and ordered a half-bottle of an excellent champagne. An older woman who looked like she was probably at the end of her shift brought it up and popped it for me out in the hall. I refused to be disappointed by her perfunctory attitude, by her tiredness, by her not being like the winking young men who brought the coffee. So I thanked her grandly and after she left, drank the whole thing on the balcony looking out over the lake. M was at a work party and I had planned to have him find me with the champagne, with the last sip maybe, still between my lips. Like, oh-there-you-are, and-here-I-was-having-a-really-absolutely-fine-time-on-my-own, but he didn't come back until long after I had drunk every drop. Until I was half asleep on the sofa.

Who was there? I asked him, sleep-whispering. Oh everyone, he said. You should have come, he said. The hotel had babysitters of course, I could have gone to the party, had even maybe been expected to. But how could I have left E or B with someone I didn't know? A hotel nanny with a plastic name-tag pinned to her shirt who didn't know how they liked to be tucked into bed, how E liked the sheet tight against her chin and how B liked to be rocked and rocked.

M's shirt, when he leaned down to kiss me, smelled of a hundred different perfumes. He slipped a hand down my back but I was already asleep.

The next morning we left for the apartment. We're going home! I told E and tried to make her feel that, that we were. M had taken the morning off, and when we left the hotel E stood in between us, holding both of our hands. On our way out I saw the same woman who had brought me the champagne the night before wheeling a cleaning trolley down the hall. I smiled at her but if she saw me she didn't show it.

M spent the whole morning moving things around the apartment until I liked it, pushing the sofa this way and that while I looked on, squinting, trying to find the perfect place. We went to IKEA together and ate hot dogs and M looked so wonderful with mustard stuck to the side of his mouth and we talked seriously-not-seriously about the kinds of wine glasses we should buy and how many we needed and what it would be like when E spoke French. A driver came to pick us up, to drop me and E and B off at the apartment and to take M back to the office. The driver held the door open for me and I slipped into the car and sitting there in the parking lot for one second the inside, the inside of the car I mean, the cool leather seats, the dark sloping dome of the roof, it all felt like bienvenue madame. It felt like it was all for me.

2

The weather had been wonderful in June. Now though it was July and we were in the apartment and summer was dragging us through its belly. We could have been the pulpy carcasses of goats swallowed whole by a crocodile. It was that hot inside the apartment. M was always gone. I found his undershirts on the floor and washed them, put his socks away and left dinners for him on the counter if I thought he might be back after we went to sleep. If I was finding everything to be harder than I had thought I might find it, well, I told myself, M was working hard too. I knew he was working so hard and everything would be easier for him, and more equal really, if everything at home was perfect and dinner was cooked well and left ready for him.

Things were going well for M's company. Money was putting down roots and growing and growing inside all of the company's accounts. Fields of fresh green data promised happiness to come. Everything was budding, bright and young and green. There were a lot of people to meet and shake hands with. M was travelling and travelling and shaking hands and every time he shook someone's hand he became more like the person he was becoming. The person in a room who could be taken at a glance to be someone in charge of things, of people, of money.

London. Berlin. Rome. I couldn't keep up really. I had trouble remembering when he was gone, and when he wasn't gone but was at the office. Really, I had trouble telling the difference. He dropped packets of candy from where he'd been on the kitchen counter for E. That's how we could tell he'd been away. How we could tell that he was back. The candy packets in the kitchen, with all their beautiful colours and amazing names. Jolly Jellies! Blumen-Zauber. Bombottini. We ate them all, E and me, all the packets. We ate every last thing he brought home and licked the sugar, le sucre, lo zucchero, den Zucker from our fingers, de nos doigts, dalle nostre dita, von unseren Fingern, like baby monsters.

It wasn't as if we weren't very busy, E and B and me. How could we not have been? There was so much to do. I signed up for a fidelity card at the dry cleaners down the street and bought a special zip-up bag with a built-in hanger for trans-porting M's suits back and forth. I deliberated as to the various ways that I should request his jackets, pants and shirts be handled, wrote carefully down sentences that could be repeated to the brisk lady at the shop. But of course I stum-bled instantly in front of her when I tried to read the script, tripping up over all the intricate sounds required to say, I would like. And we would end with me only silently nodding, silently thank-you smiling, and her sniffing and handing me a receipt.

M was always away one way or another. He was always gone. The apartment door was shut behind him each morning when we woke and that was good and fine really. He was getting on with things and we were left inside to our own devices. How wonderful I told E, how wonderfully lucky we are to be free like this, free to do exactly as we please.

We slept all the time, E and me and B, and sometimes we didn't sleep at all. Time was inconvenient, unpredictable. Sometimes it rushed me along and sometimes the minutes wrapped themselves around me, pressing, expecting to be entertained like children, needing something, needing to be fed, as if the hours were animals opening their mouths, the endless parade of minutes lodging like tiny bones in a thousand soft throats. The light never changed. I studied the coins M left on the bedside table like artefacts, his water glasses, the wet towels he left on the floor. I slipped my hand inside all of his pockets before I took his clothes to the cleaners. Perhaps he thought of me too, perhaps we were each of us ghosts to each other. Boo, I could whisper maybe in his ear while he slept. Here I am.

Every morning I sat by the water pump in the little park, watching E splash, arranging the blanket over B so it would shade him. I spent what felt like, what really could have been, years washing the sand off E's feet. She on the blanket with B, me running back and forth to the pump for handfuls of water, searching between her toes. I'm a crab! I'd say, walking sideways, holding my arms up in the air. We polished the tools too and rubbed the handles clean.

In the afternoons sometimes I called my mother. Look at this! I would say and show her something or other. A picture E had drawn maybe or a tracing of B's hand. Look! And of course it was all amazing. Open a window, my mother would say. I can't see anything. She would ask about M and the answer was always that he was at work. Well he was. And what about you, she said. But there never was much time to talk. There was always so much to do, so much to get done. Au revoir, I'd say to her. What's that? she'd say.

One morning, while I ran to the pump, my keys were stolen. I'd given them to B to suck on, but, when I got back, B was holding a handful of sticks and grass and my keys were gone. I got down on my hands and knees and crawled all around the blanket looking for them, but they had vanished. I asked E what had happened but she only shrugged, as if keys and all such grown-up nonsense were quite beneath her and B only burbled and blew bubbles and was generally no help at all. I felt maybe like shrieking, but of course I didn't. I just looked again and again and again in the grass, clicking my tongue and circling the edge of our blanket like a spider spinning a web, or like those seeds that drop, spiralling from the maples each fall. Going round and round like that.

I couldn't ask the other people at the park what had happened, I didn't have the words. Bonjour, I could say. Merci. But of course those weren't the words I wanted. There was usually some way to make everything better, but sometimes there wasn't. I made a note to myself to learn the word for help.

I thought of the door to the apartment, locked firm and fast and me and E and B on the wrong side of it. I thought of how cool the rooms might be mid-morning, with the shutters still shut against the sun, our beds all unmade, undone and scrumptious, the covers spilling this way and that and ready to have us back again. I felt such a sinking then, without the keys, without any way back into that place where E and B and I could be alone together. It was like a hole opened up, there in the park, there in the ground underneath me.

B began to fuss and I picked him up and held him close. The bedroom windows looked out onto the park from behind a little fence and I gazed at them almost hungrily. That's when I noticed. The bedroom window, my bedroom window, was slightly open. Just a crack, but big enough I thought to slip through. I shoved all our things together, horribly jumbled into my bag, and ran over to the fence. It was a little fence, easy to get over, but still there, marking something. A neighbour's yard perhaps, but it ran right beneath my bedroom window. I hesitated, but then we were all suddenly there at the window and I was lifting E up and setting her inside the apartment and climbing in myself, one hand pressed against the back of B's soft baby head to steady him. I was actually breathing hard from relief, and I felt tears prick my eyes and wondered what it was I'd been so afraid of at the park. After all, keys were only keys, I could get new ones. Shakily I made my way to the kitchen to get myself a glass of water and found, beside the cooktop, my keys. Set there so sweetly as if waiting for me, as if they had been returned. There's a word for that in French. Coming home, and maybe, in French, anything could do it, come home I mean. *Les clés sont rentrées.* I ran and checked the front door to see if I had somehow left it open, if everything could be explained in that way, but it was locked.

In the afternoon I walked to the fruit market, one hand in E's hand, the other pushing B's stroller. Words flew by all around me, like flocks of birds, feathers and wings, filling my vision brightly but leaving nothing for me to touch.

I pointed at baskets of blackberries, tomatoes the size of champagne bubbles, wheels of cheese. By opening my hands wider or narrowing the space between them, I could ask for more or for less. E ran off, disappearing into the crowd, and came back to me with the pockets of her little blue dress filled with apricots.

Back at the apartment, we ate at the kitchen table. I sliced blackberries the size of B's fist. The apricots were soft, fuzz-covered fontanelles, we chomped them up greedily, the warm juice staining our necks. The afternoon went on and on inside the apartment. M was travelling. I tried to call my mother but I couldn't find my phone. Look at us! I said to E. All alone!

After it was dark, I crept out the front door, and locked it, checking that I had the keys in my pocket. E and B, I left sleeping in their beds. With M gone there was no one to take out the garbage. Really, I was doing a necessary thing. I lingered by the bins. Sorting papers, pulling the plastic film from boxes, slipping the slick pits of apricots one by one into the compost. Touching everything. B might wake up at any moment. E might. Any moment was a moment they might wake and find me gone.

There were people across the street, sitting at the precarious cafe tables. A woman, alone, and a few men at a table behind her sipping wine from tiny glasses. My fingers were sticky from the apricot pits. The woman wore a long wool coat despite the heat. Her white hair was pinned into a complicated arrangement. She reached into her purse and began counting out coins, laying them piece by piece on the table next to her cup. Each coin looked like it had been polished at home, maybe she too had minutes, hours, time overflowing. Long afternoons. A waiter collected her money but she made no move to leave. Instead she put a cigarette to her lips, struck a match and lit it and settled back into her chair. She wasn't waiting for anyone. She wasn't going anywhere. She would, maybe, sit there smoking all night.

I hurried back to the apartment. The children were still asleep. I rinsed my hands. I wondered about my phone. Tried to find it again, couldn't. Tried to remember the notes I wrote to myself on it. Milk! Toilet paper! All the bookmarked pages filled with the various protocols I had been advised to keep always accessible. What signs of shock might result from a bee sting. What to do after a blow to the head. What to do for a burn, or for an even worse burn, what to do then. What to do in case of choking. CPR chest compression numbers. Thirty pumps and then a rescue breath.

My mother saved my life once, with a phone, with a phone call that is. I was maybe two, in the bathtub, playing in the water, and she'd fallen asleep on the floor next to me. She must have been so terrified when she woke up and found me. You were blue under the water, you were just like those swimming-pool tiles, she always said, when she told the story. Blue! Then she'd say, Why didn't you wake me up? Why didn't you scream or splash around, or something, she'd say, Jesus. You just let yourself slip under. Phones were screwed into the walls then and she'd been able to call 911. She'd been able to put her fingers on the right buttons and find a person on the other end of the line when she'd needed, really needed, to scream for help. Help!

Always have your phone, she'd told me after E was born. Her one piece of advice. Ohforgoodnesssake, she'd say if she tried to call me now and I didn't pick up. Well, it was stuck maybe between the couch cushions. It could have been any old place. I curled up beside E in her bed and went to sleep.

*

The next morning B woke up early and then we all did. There was no yogurt so we had to go out. The sidewalk was already too hot. We walked so slowly. E sometimes stopped altogether. B was sweating in his bassinet. It was such a short distance to the store. I could have flown there in ten heartbeats if I'd been a bird. I felt myself becoming unreasonable. I was unhappy with the way I was dressed, with my uncombed hair, my lips, barnacled with dead skin, were like tide pools. E stopped to watch a man wash the concrete in front of another building. Everything was always being scrubbed clean here. The concierge wiped my fingerprints off the front of the mailbox every morning after I checked it for letters.

I felt my breath begin to catch in my throat. I was beginning to sweat. I pulled E towards the store, harder than I meant to, and she began to cry. We only need two tubs of yogurt! I said to her, as if this could have explained everything. At the store E was mad at me but I made my best horrible face at her and said Boo! and she laughed and we were friends again.

When we got home there was a bouquet of flowers lying on the doorstep. Aurelie, the card said in beautiful looping fountain-pen French. The letters looked delicate, as if eyelashes had just happened to fall in that particular pattern on the page. I looked up and down the hall in front of the apartment door but there was no one there. There was no one there to tell me that these flowers weren't meant for me. I grabbed them. The petals were cool against my cheek, cool and remote. As if they had only just now appeared in the world. I filled a vase with water and settled the flowers inside. There was nowhere in the apartment to put them. They were that marvellous.

What does the card say? E asked me. Who are the flowers for? Wondering perhaps, whether they were for me, or for her.

They are for the Princess Aurelie, I told her, inventing. Who lives in a white castle with golden gates. We're keeping them for her, I said, here with us.

When will she come and get them? E asked, watching me.

In the middle of the night, I told her. Princess Aurelie will come and get them when we're all asleep.

There was an Aurelie though, a real Aurelie out there with arms and legs who sometimes got flowers given to her that were beautiful. Flowers that were just like these flowers, from someone who liked to imagine her at her doorstep, bending at the waist, picking them up.

I unpacked the bag from the market and discovered it was full of tram tickets. There must have been at least twelve of them, all time stamped with the date, today, and the time, right now. They were all good for an hour of travel on any bus, tram or water taxi in the city of Geneva. Handfuls of opportunities, there in fresh ink. Coffee on the Île Rousseau, macaroons at Ladurée, shopping or a dip in the wading pools at the Jardin Botanique. Anything.

It was just that I couldn't remember stopping at the ticket machine. I could recall nothing of filling my bag with long strings of useless tickets. E and B ate the tiny tubs of yogurt. They were so fresh that they tasted like meadow grass. We ate them all up, one two three and so on, gobbling.

After breakfast I washed E's hair and dried it with her favourite towel. I cut B's nails and packed our bag for the park. The beautiful red tools. A purple watering can for the plants. Crackers, cucumber slices, a hunk of cheese. Simply getting ourselves to the little park behind our apartment was momentous.

E wasn't helping and B was crying again. I thought maybe I would shout, Put your shoes on! Or else, Where is your other shoe! Or, Where is your hat! Then, suddenly and inexplicably and just like that, I was crying. I was holding B and my diaper bag and my beautifully packed snacks and toys in the hallway and crying in front of the door, and I found that my face was wet and also my hands from wiping my eyes and also my neck and the front of my shirt and B was looking at me and E was, and there we all were and there was no way to explain.

We threw a party when we left, M and me, for all our friends, to celebrate. His new job, our new lives, all of it. A real dinner party in our house, after he signed the contract and before it was empty, the house I mean. When we were still surrounded by everything that we loved and everything too that we were leaving. We threw a party and so many people came that finally M shouted, Leave the door open, just leave it, and I cooked salmon that was pink inside like kisses and we opened so many bottles of wine.

As a child, I had been obsessed with stories of covered wagons. The Wild West. Wagon trains riding off into the sunset. Children walking all the way to California. They moved so slowly, the wagon trains, that each night they were within sight of the place that they had camped the night before. I hadn't been able to imagine it then, but now, of course, I understood how one could see easily places that can never be returned to. It could all be right before your eyes.

That evening I recycled the tram tickets, wrapping them in the paper the flowers had come in. Yellow lemony tissue. I threw it all into the bins.

3

There was a problem with my new Swiss credit card. It was cracked a little, just across the security chip. It was almost invisible, the crack, but in the end it didn't matter that it was so small because I couldn't use the card to buy things or to make withdrawals at the ATM. I kept having to ask M for money. He'd leave it for me on the counter and I'd use it to buy food or little presents for E when we were out. But I wanted to take things into my own hands as it were, and one morning I wrapped B in his swaddling blanket and set him all businesslike in his stroller and took E's hand and we rode the tram into Geneva to go to the bank.

I showed my broken card at reception and an assistant led me into a private waiting room that was very white and had a large paper chandelier swanning down into the middle of it. E wanted to touch it and I did too but I told her no. B began to fuss in his stroller and I got him out to nurse him. I had my shirt hitched up and me everywhere out in the room when the assistant came back with the obligatory thimble of espresso and he was so startled that he dropped the cup. Of course this brought the cleaning crew but by then B was finished nursing and I set him smacking his lips and sleepy back into his stroller for a nap. I tucked my shirt back into my skirt and the assistant brought a second cup of coffee and we both avoided looking at each other while I took it and thanked him.

In the end though, there was nothing they could do for me at the bank. They said it like that, in beautiful English, over and over again. The account manager, the director and the managing director of the department. There is nothing we can do to help you. I kept asking to talk to someone else, but in the end there wasn't anyone else. I spilled my wallet out and picked up all the pieces: my cards, my ID. This is me, I said. But the problem was, I wasn't on the account. I was tired, B hadn't been sleeping and I couldn't, just really couldn't think through what they were saying to me, the manager, the director and the managing director. For an instant I almost really went toppling over, my vision suddenly blurring, filling with the shapes of their faces, all smiling politely and nodding at me.

It was my residence permit, they told me. It wasn't entirely complete, there was some stamp or other that needed stamping. Or, I had a different sort of permit that didn't allow me to open bank accounts. I really couldn't understand. Anyway I couldn't be named on the account, they said, smiling at me, nodding at me, and instead M had opened the account in his name and given me a card for it. He must have forgotten to tell me, or been embarrassed to. I was embarrassed, there at the bank, with all my useless cards spread out on the table, and my sagging diaper bag and bottles and snacks jumbled and awful and taking up all their clean white space. But you can use the card of course, said the account manager, smiling, flicking her long hair back over her shoulder, even though it's not in your name. But I can't, I said, use the card. They offered me a second cup of coffee.

We left the bank and walked over to the lake and up to the pier where the Jet d'Eau shoots up and out of the water and you can feel the spray on your face and we did, feel it. We spread out our arms and turned in circles with all the other people who were visiting the city. Just feeling all that water land so lightly on our faces.

M was home and M was gone again. He called the bank and ordered me a new credit card. It's so dumb, he said, that I couldn't put you on the account. I meant to tell you. We'll fix it later, he said. When I'm not so busy at work. We'll figure something out. Sorry about this, I said. No problem, he said, really. Let me know if there's anything else. No, I said, it's OK.

Maybe we were residents of different countries now, me and M. There was, at least, an ocean of paperwork between us, stamps, seals, phone numbers to call, people to reach that could not be reached. Different kinds of permits permitting different kinds of things. Our credit cards were almost identical to look at, but of course that meant very little, or really that meant nothing at all.

As a girl I learned SOS in Morse code. I could flash it with a flashlight or rap it with my knuckles on a wall or counter. I could even signal it with my eyelids, with the way I blinked. In case a stranger took me by the hand and tried to make me get in his car, I could blink for help surreptitiously. I suppose, the main thing about what I assumed, was that someone would be there to come when I needed it, would be there watching me, waiting for my signal even. The trick, I must have thought, was only to know the right way to ask.

When I was a girl, I was often involved one way or another in elaborate games. They were like boats, the games, that sailed me from here to there, between the minutes, safely from one hour to the next. One summer my favourite game was called Flash-Flood. In the game I was stranded, alone, on a beautiful island. Everywhere the ground was carpeted with dry grass and beautiful flowers. In the middle of the island was a tree with a treehouse that could be accessed by a narrow wooden ladder.

During the game I would be the girl and the girl would pick flowers until suddenly, the girl would see a flash flood. Which is to say she would see water coming at her from a distance, rushing at terrible, even impossible speeds. The girl would scream. The girl was at all times both tragic and beautiful. The girl would fling her flowers down and run for the ladder and always she would pull herself up at the very last possible moment. Always the bottom of the shoe of the last foot into the treehouse would get wet. The point was to get to safety, but the point was also I suppose, thinking about it now, that the girl always did. That somehow, the girl always knew when to fling down the flowers and run. The right way to ask, the right exact moment to run away. Safety was always possible but it hinged on codes, secret knowledge and precision. The girl could save herself but only if she did everything right.

The flowers in the vase were dead now. Where is the Princess? E asked, looking at the flowers. Why didn't she come? We both thought that maybe she'd been eaten by trolls, we both agreed that this was horrible. To myself though, I thought, that someone must send the real Aurelie flowers every day, that she must have vases overflowing and a path of petals leading from the flower shop to her apartment. To myself I thought that these flowers, my flowers, were, to her, to Aurelie, a drop in the bucket, nothing that she would miss or come looking for.

Anyway, they were hanging down over the top of the rental-company vase, their heads drying, the stalks melting slowly into goo, disappearing into the brackish water. I could never remember to get rid of them and so we, E, B and I, watched the deterioration. We noted the smells that rose from the water, the rot creeping up the stems. It was science, I told E. E took her animals, two plastic giraffes, a mother and a baby, one orphaned kangaroo, a baby orangutan and a white pony with dark spots, one by one to the edge of the vase to sniff the water. To gaze into it. Some of the fallen petals were collected to make a nest for the kangaroo. We were learning now by watching very carefully. Look, I said to her. Look at this and this and this.

I wasn't sleeping, I really wasn't. Not much. Not enough. E got up early. B stayed up late. In between the nights stretched, the hours drifting farther and farther from each other, like planets pushing outwards, always more and more alone inside the expanding dark. M was back sometimes and sleeping but he felt always very far away. When he didn't come home I called my mother from the guest room and I'd gaze at the screen and not be able to make any sense of what she was saying. Go to sleep, she'd say, you look awful.

The days melted into each other. I felt it overwhelming sometimes that I was expected, all the time, to be a person. I woke in pieces. I was a random collection of parts. One shoulder but not the other, one ear. The skin on my face was raw, peeled open. I was so tired that it was really like that. It won't last I thought. This is a phase, this is only now and now isn't always. This minute is only this minute and this minute is only one minute long. Sometimes I would hang myself in the doorway, like a bat, with my arms and shoulders held at odd, rigid angles, and I would say Boo! to E when she came around the corner. Look! I would say, I'm a bat!

Come be my bat baby, come be my baby bat and she would laugh and I would hug her little reed-body and wish suddenly, sharply, for this minute we were in to last for ever.

My hands were raw from washing dishes, from grappling with the unmanageable weight of wet laundry, from soaping hair, and brushing teeth. One night, I came back to myself with a start. It must have been two or three in the morning, one of those hours between children, when the apartment seemed to have no one but myself inside it. I found myself standing by the door, my hand on the door handle, my bag on my shoulder. I threw the bag down and tram tickets, whole streams of them, waterfalled out in a rush of paper, the ink black and fresh and gleaming, the paper curling around my ankles like inviting foam. I ran to check on B.

He was asleep in his crib and I woke him, shaking his shoulder a bit, my wet fingers leaving prints on his soft little sleeping shirt. Once he was awake he wanted me. I picked him up and shushed him. I settled with him on the sofa and slipped my nipple into his mouth for him to suck. There, I said, there, there, there. I'm here, I said. Here I am.

Afterwards, satisfied, I put him back down and I crawled into my own bed and we were all good and quiet then. Tucked in and up and away, each of us under our own clean sheets we were right in our right places and ready for M to sweetly find us, to kiss our cheeks when he came home, whenever it was that he did.

4

The next day came and found us though, in the early morning hours. B was hungry and we passed driftingly around the dining table, sitting down for just a minute in each place, the only guests at the party, sitting alone together in all the various chairs.

I wanted to make the empty room into a guest room. A really really perfect guest room. Everything would be white, I could see it, really see it in my head the way it would be. Towels, bedspread, pillow cases, sheets and curtains. Light and white. Glowing and scrubbed clean. Inside, everything would drift lazily, like on the best summer days.

I wanted sheets for that room that were so bright and clean that it would make anyone who slept there feel encompassed, touched, free. Like she would wake every morning with the sun on her face. There was a part of me that really believed sheets could do that, could make someone feel that way.

A bed would barely fit inside the little room, but that was all right, it would be like a ship. The way they look when they're being built, when they're girded and trussed in the yard. The bed would be like that in the little room. Hulking and wooden, well-outfitted with its prow pointed towards summer. What I'm trying to say is how deeply I imagined it, the room.

The only thing was the soap. I couldn't see it. There must be soap to sit on the edge of the little sink in a white cup and the soap should be wrapped in a paper that was not white, paper of the most perfect colour. Something that would explain everything, keep the ship afloat, the white of the curtains billowing. Calm seas, white sand, warm sun. I couldn't see it yet though. I couldn't see that little part.

I was sitting on the grey rental-company sofa holding B as he fought off sleep, his small hands curling, as if digging himself out of a pit. As night turned into morning, I could feel the heat rising in the room, the sun beginning to boil the metal shutters, but I didn't get up to open a window. He eventually drifted off making a little sound like a balloon does when it's losing air and I fell asleep holding him, and woke to E's eyes, held right up close to mine. Wake up, she said, wake up. Her animals were arranged in a ring around my feet, there were so many little painted plastic eyes looking at me. They're hungry, E said.

We fed the animals sesame seeds. I made coffee. The smell of the beans tangled with the sweet rot from the flowers.

The tram tickets in my bag, all stamped with yesterday's date and good for an hour of travel in the middle of the night, I swept into a drawer in the kitchen with the other tickets, with all the things I meant to think about later, when there was time.

The heat crept into the apartment. It crept into our mouths and made our tongues too thick to lick our gummy teeth. We floated in pools of our own sweat, drifting as if we were holidaymakers floating down the lazy river on those swarms of plastic tubes. Let's turn off the lights, I said to E. Let's keep the shutters closed. Let's make it dark inside and maybe that will keep away the heat. E liked it I think, so we let the ceilings hang over us like low clouds.

At the store, I attempted to make sense of the different detergents. Bottles to make towels soft, to remove spots of various kinds, to make whites white. Maybe they were for that, I didn't know really. I couldn't read any of the words. In the meat aisle E poked the dead, broken-necked chickens, each displayed on his or her own, individual styrofoam tray. Their plucked skin was the most beautiful pearly pink. E wanted to buy them, to cook them or love them for ever I couldn't tell. Anyway it didn't matter because I couldn't touch them, could almost not go near them even, it seemed too brutal, to be on a tray like that, to be pressed and wrapped into it, unable to move. It seemed like something that was happening, it seemed urgent somehow to me then that under all their graceful wrappings it would have been impossible to breathe.

40

In the afternoon I hung the laundry all around the house, and E and I pretended we lived in a forest, where all the children had, one day, quite suddenly and with no warning flown away, leaving only all their clothes, hanging on the branches. Weee we whispered to each other from among the branches, swinging.

At the park, I began to watch another mother with her children. She also came most afternoons to sit by the pump. She had a baby, a boy, maybe six months old, that she wore snuggled in one of those complicated wraps. She seemed to spin into and out of it, the wrap, without trouble, as if love made such a thing easy. She had another child, also a boy, about E's age, who walked beside her along the clipped green hedges that lined the park, his hand in her hand, the space between them so lovely, like a garden, like a kingdom between their hips.

She carried her things easily, her bags I mean. A blanket for the baby, the toy the older child particularly wanted, snacks, a yellow washcloth, water bottles. She spoke with her baby as if they were in constant conversation, meeting his eyes, making him laugh. Rolling a ball to him over and over as if she could never tire of it. Singing to him. Leaving him easily, to push her son on the swing, to find his truck, to fill a bucket with water as if this was no trouble. Well, I was fascinated by all of it, the way she moved, the way she was, the way she loved them. I drank it up, maybe, is the way to say what I did, what I was doing watching her at the park. Drinking.

She was beautiful, her face was like a collection of interesting things arranged perfectly along the high shelf of her cheekbones. Arranged, as if to say look at this, or this, or this. A long nose, thick eyebrows, one crooked tooth. There was some wildness about her that I couldn't place. That made me look back at her wondering. I couldn't tell if her quiet poise meant calm or terror. I couldn't tell what kind of animal she was.

Men walking past the park would catch their eyes on her. They would get caught up and tangled like that, for a second, for a half a second. Fathers meeting their children in the park after work would hesitate for one heartbeat maybe, at the edge of her blanket, as if they'd just then remembered dropping something.

She never looked up though, at the hesitating heart-stopped fathers. She wouldn't have. I knew she wouldn't have. I watched the way she held the ball she tossed to her baby, the way she pushed her boy in a swing, the way she took her son's hand as they walked, so I felt I knew these things. I called her Nell, to myself, inside my head, when I thought about her. She smiled at me once, and I smiled back. She had the most delightful gap between two of her teeth, not her front ones. See? I could have said to her. See? Who we are? Who could reproach us? Who could think a single bad thought about us? We who are doing the most beautiful thing in the world.

When E was born, when we brought her home from the

hospital, I was so overwhelmed with love that I wanted to speak to her in a different language. A language apart from the everyday chatter that carried on all around us, that I'd heard all my life. I wanted to speak to her in a language that existed only for the two us. I loved her like that, that much. Sometimes love is like that though, it can be blind and demanding, it can be such a beautiful trap.

At the park if E and B were happy for a moment I brought out my book, *Easy French*, and tried to make sense of the words. I read over the dialogues, mouthing out the words to simple questions. Trips to the pharmacy, the library, a movie theatre and the park. I tried to remember the answers characters gave to the questions they were constantly being asked. I tried to formulate answers to imaginary questions that someone might ask me. I tried to find it, the thread that would string the words together, the thread that could knit me into the afternoon.

How old is your baby? someone could ask me. Where do you live? Where is the supermarket? I am thirty-four years old, I could say. I have two children. A boy and a girl, I could say. My hair is brown. My hair is short. My eyes are blue and green and grey. Each word I could puzzle out was a victory, something plucked from the abyss, from the edge of the world. A marvel.

In my apartment I thought about Nell. I thought about her in her apartment, about the closet she must hang her long dresses in, about the places she settled her children down to sleep. How she must iron their pillowcases, hang their bath toys to dry so mould would never grow inside them. How mould would never ever grow anywhere inside her house. How she must have tucked the hours all around her boys, fluffing pillows, smoothing hair, making every minute seem secure. I pictured her living in a house perched high on a hill above the tram stop where everything was green and frothy with light, where the breeze always blew very gently through the yellow-draped windows. Aurelie with her flowers, Nell with her children, petals and soft cheeks, I could see them perfectly, in their perfect homes.

I didn't have a job, not anymore. Afterwards, after E was born, after I quit, well, it was as if I had woken up on a very quiet island. An island where it was always afternoon and I was alone, alone with E. We could have made a raft, rowed somewhere. I could have, but where would we have gone?

Sometimes I yelled then, when she was a baby, just to make all the quiet disappear for a while. To push it back and away from us. All that quiet, all those hours, just her and me in our old house, looking out on our old street. Sometimes we'd just yell together and hold hands.

M was going to leave on a trip, he'd be gone for two weeks. There was a big conference and then some meetings. Some of the other wives were going to a mountain house, he told me, a real chalet-type thing. He wanted me to go. There was a sandy beach on a lake, he said. A boat for E to play in, other children, green meadows and flowers in window boxes, cows with cowbells. Real Swiss stuff, he said. You could get some help maybe, he said, with the kids. Two weeks is a long time to be on your own. It might be good to have some company, you all could help each other out.

But we were fine here, I told him. Besides, I told him, there wasn't such a thing as holidays for mothers, or holidays from mothering for that matter. So why pretend we could go somewhere to get a break. I didn't want to go and mother with the other mothers at the lake. We'd choke each other. We'd be like seals piling our ungainly motherbodies one on top of the other. No, thank you, I didn't need any bit of that. Mothering is a hard job, it needs a lot of space to breathe. Really, I didn't want to travel, I only wanted to sleep.

The morning M left I got up with him and walked him to the door. He wheeled his Samsonite between us, a garment bag slung over his arm with miles and miles of beautiful suits zipped up inside it. He checked his phone and told me the date he'd be back, I circled it on the little calendar the rental company had given us. Love Geneva in July, it said, and there was a big red heart drawn over a picture of the shining lake. Swans, mountains. M was going to be gone until the end of it, until the end of the month.

Kiss E and B for me, he said. Be good. I don't know about the hours, he said, when I'll be able to call, it's going to be really busy. It's OK, I said. Don't worry about us. We'll be fine. You'll do great. But when I said that, You'll do great, I suddenly felt a kind of confusion. Wrongfooted is the way I felt, as if I'd tripped, vastly. Because of course how was I to know anything about what he was doing and how he would do it. He fumbled with his wallet, his keys, leaned over to kiss me. Sometimes everything was the same and sometimes things were different. When he kissed me for example. Just leave the door open, he'd said, at the party that we'd thrown together, just leave it, when I'd cooked salmon that was pink inside like kisses and we'd opened so many bottles of wine.

He tried to reach around me, to pull me in closer, but business cards scattered out of his pocket like sudden snow. They were so beautiful, the cards. They really were. The printed letters were like vertebrae, each one delicate, embossed, polished to a high shine. I bent to pick them up but the taxi was already outside. I have cards too! I wanted to shout, joking-not-joking, I have cards too, my pockets are stuffed with them. They say unconditional love and they are ready upon demand. They are ready for anyone to ask to see them. The door was already closed behind him though, he was already gone. I stacked up his cards neatly and put them by the door. When he came back, he would find them there.

5

The days grew hotter and hotter. Soon it was too hot to eat anything but lemons. We squeezed the juice over sugar and ice. I stopped cooking. Even boiling water for pasta could not be done. Instead I bought bags and bags of lemons at the market. I walked up and down the stalls, between the laden tables, pulling E, pushing B. In the apartment we stacked the lemons in bowls, crowding the small kitchen table with gleaming yellow towers of fruit. B loved to play with them, their intoxicating shapes, he would bat at them if I put them on the floor and send them rolling. He had a tooth now and he loved to sink it right into their bright delightful rinds.

I liked to have a bowl of lemons in the guest room. The best bowl, the best lemons. I dragged one of the rental-company chairs into the little room and set the bowl on it. The chair was the wrong colour, but the lemons, the idea of them, was right. It was so hot though, in there, that the lemons turned to rot. Always, almost within hours, they broke out in a pulpy grey fuzz and I would have to take them out and throw them away.

The fruit seller, a large woman with sunburnt hands and a faded apron, began to know me. She began to nod at me when I arrived at her table in the afternoons. It felt like an achievement. It really did! Well, what more could one achieve really? I was careful to nod back at her, moving my head exactly as much as she did. I didn't want to seem stand-offish but neither did I want to appear overeager.

One afternoon she gave E a paper carton of glistening red berries. Back at the apartment we tasted them together, dipping them one by one into a bowl of ice-cold cream while the baby slept. We licked our fingers. We popped the berries between our teeth. With children the future is always unimaginable, it is so uncertain as to be nothing. Less than that. As a mother, I had had to learn that, that the only sweetness you're ever guaranteed, the full extent, is right now, the moment right between your teeth.

The next day I steered E to a different table to buy the lemons. I was worried the woman would think we expected another gift. It was so hard, it was always so hard to know what was right. I nodded at the lady as we passed though and she nodded back at me.

I began to fall asleep sometimes. Sometimes when I didn't mean to I mean. I would just wink out like a candle, like the shutter of a camera closing, and then, click the shutter would open and I would find E staring at me as if she'd asked a question and I hadn't answered her. Or as if I had answered her and the answer hadn't been right. Anyway, I began to be afraid that I might fall asleep and E might wander off, out of the apartment, without me. So I began to remind myself always to lock the apartment door when we were inside. B was beginning to crawl a bit so I also began to lock the windows. It was just a question of practicality, of having to outsmart myself because, well, I couldn't quite trust myself. Not all the time. It made the apartment hotter, the locked windows, but it seemed the only way to keep us all safe, at least until M was back and I could sleep properly. At least until then.

B was tired too. He hated the heat. He cried in his bassinet and pulled at the sweaty baby curls behind his ears. E had lines of salt criss-crossing the back of her shirt like the shadows of prehistoric sea creatures, ammonites I told her.

Mostly I squeezed lemons and spooned sugar into cups. It was OK when we ran out of ice. It's OK, I told E, it's better. In the desert they would never think of drinking cold drinks. They really wouldn't! Look at us, here in this heat, drinking warm lemonade. Look at us!

Once, E reached for her cup too soon, while I was still squeezing and measuring and pouring, lemon and sugar and water, and the sticky sweet juice spilled on the counter, on the floor. That's OK! I said. That's OK! Look, we can clean it up, and I was smiling. All we have to do is get this towel wet, and kneel down on the floor and find every little drop. We can do that, I said. We can be so clean and tidy and good. There was so much smiling to do. So much teaching and smiling and not minding. Wiping and drying, sorting, smiling and not mindingabit.

One afternoon I took B over to the sofa to feed him. I let him settle into the crook of my arm and I suppose I fell asleep. Anyway I woke with a start. I woke with B's sleeping body sliding off my chest, towards the dangerous cushions. My heart leapt. It was as if I was dangling his small body over the edge of a ravine. It really was like that.

I had been told terrible stories of mothers who allowed themselves to fall asleep in this way, with their babies drifting helplessly towards the cushions. If we slept, we mothers, we slept cheek to cheek with disaster. That close, with terror touching us and singing to us in our dreams.

I couldn't catch my breath. There wasn't enough air. My face felt tight. I put B down in his crib next to the sofa and ran to the bathroom. My face was a riot of colours, blues streaked down my cheek from the corner of my eye down to my collarbone. Thick red paste was caked around my lips in circles that had been drawn and redrawn again and again. My eyelids were silver, bulging out of my face, like the hard backs of beetles.

E was behind me, smiling. Pretty she said. When I looked down at the sink I saw that my make-up bag was open. Lipstick, brushes, sponges, powders, paints. Expensive liquids of all different colours dripped from the mouths of tiny vials. The sink was stained, the towels were stained, the rental company's perfect walls.

I smiled back at E out of my cakey mouth. There was lipstick sticking to my tongue and teeth. Pretty, I said. Yes, it's pretty! Spelled, P-r-e-t-t-y. I spelled the letters with my fingers in the air. We played all afternoon with the shutters drawn. I kept my eyes on B, trying to breathe, trying to see him breathe, feeling the ceiling right on top of us all the time.

That night, after B and E had fallen asleep, I scrubbed my face, and cleaned up the wreckage in the bathroom, all the ruined tubes, the lipsticks, the tiny blush boxes. I picked up too, the whole apartment. Starting in one room and moving through all the others slowly. Our games had taken over the place a bit. Crept up on us, encroached. I hadn't noticed. Or I had noticed and had let myself loose, had tried to, as if I were glossy green leaves floating in water and could be beautiful and delicate and wavering and touched just here and here, just dappled maybe in the right light. But now, cleaning, I saw it. The mess, the games, the importance of not wavering.

There was the egg carton on the counter, split open with the shells all jumbled up inside it, the cups and dishes from the tea party we'd had on the floor. There were the bits and bobs we'd brought in from the park and stowed in E's bed. The sticks and apple cores. The secrets. The treasures. The wooden music box we'd found by the bins, that E had loved and that we'd brought back with us, dancing into the apartment, and that I now saw was speckled at the joints with mould. The doll we'd found in the sandbox with the broken neck. I filled bag after bag with the remnants of our marvellous games. The lemons in the guest room had rotted spectacularly, they turned almost to dust in my hands. I took the bags out of the apartment two by two, to the bins, making many trips until the apartment was clean again and ready for us all to love each other better, ready for us all to love each other so much.

After my last trip, on my way back to the apartment, I saw the woman with the pinned white hair sitting outside the cafe drinking coffee. She wore the same long coat, even in the heat, the buttons done up, right up to her neck. Her polished change lay already counted, arranged on the tabletop next to her saucer. Her feet were crossed, as before, at the ankles, tucked underneath her chair as if making space for someone else to come and sit across from her.

She was dipping the corner of her napkin into the tea-light on the table, letting the flame catch and tapping it out again with her fingers. Reflexively almost, over and over, lighting it, snuffing it out. There was only a moment, each time in between lighting and snuffing, for the tiny flame to live, for it to be alive.

I took two steps towards her, I really did. Thinking maybe in my tiredness that she had arranged all this somehow, for me. Thinking that she was signalling me. Hi, I would say,

52

Bonsoir. We would have interesting things to say to each other. She would tell me about some wild thing she'd done when she was young. Some train that she'd ridden on in Russia, where the air was so cold outside that all the beautiful people inside the ice-covered carriages had to spend the whole night kissing and touching each other to stay warm. Something like that.

She let the napkin drop, stuck a cigarette between her lips and lit it. I could hear the crackling of the paper burning. She looked up then, with the cigarette stuck between her lips, and her face, facing me was different, not mysterious, just tired, lonely maybe and I saw immediately the foolishness of what I was doing. Standing in the street in my scrubbed face, waiting to be asked to sit down.

Back inside the apartment, I ran my hands over the kitchen counter and checked three times that the refrigerator was shut tight and not open at all. I sat at the table, then lay down on the kitchen floor. I closed my eyes, hoping that the hum of the refrigerator would put me to sleep. M had been gone a week and I pressed my face into the warm kitchen floor as if I were pressing it into his back. I wondered if he came home right then, if he opened the door, what he would have said, finding me there like that.

Morning came, like it does, and I was on the kitchen floor and I had been there all night and I peeled myself up off it and got on with things. My hands shook a little when I held

B. I couldn't dress him anymore, he seemed to change every minute. Sometimes he was too big for his clothes, sometimes he looked lost in them, swimming in loose fabric that could twist around his neck the moment I looked away. Every minute was capable of bringing such terrible things. I left him in his pyjamas.

E dressed herself. We got to the park early in the morning. We had the water pump all to ourselves. I had forgotten to pack the tools so E made do with her hands. Scooping the water onto the sand tiny handfuls at a time. She mounded the wet sand up around the giraffes, coaxing it into small hills, from which the giraffes, buried up to their long necks, cried for her help.

Sometimes she would rescue them right away, sometimes she would ignore them, piling the sand higher and higher, building houses, whole towns, out of sticks on top of them, and bringing smaller sticks, people, to live inside. All the sticks knew to ignore the sounds coming from underneath their feet. It hardly mattered, the water from the pump would always, eventually, wash it all away and the giraffes would be cleaned and welcomed back and tended to. Here, she would whisper to them, telling secrets in their little brown-painted plastic ears, here I am.

We played the days away and I marked them off on the calendar, all businesslike. At night I swept up all our things and cleaned as if we were expecting guests, or as if we were guests in someone else's house, it didn't matter. It took a lot of energy though, I feel I should mention, the playing and the cleaning up after. Staying on top of things. Sometimes my heart would start to beat very quickly and if E noticed or if E said, You're sweating, I was quick to make a game of it.

I kept forgetting to call my mother and when I remembered she didn't answer, or if she did the connection was bad and she would only stare at me from far away, her face frozen in its ring of light. I would stare then at the pixels and try to make out what colour eyeshadow she was wearing or what she was having for lunch. At night I would take her into the guest room and lie on the floor and talk to her. B's great, I would say. He's getting big. He's doing this or that, any baby thing. And I would wait for her lips that weren't moving to ask me, where's M. And with my lips that weren't moving I would ask her if it was possible to tell between what a man, what a husband, had to do and what he chose to do, and if *had to*, and *chose to*, changed for a husband who became an important man. With my lips that weren't moving I wanted to tell her that M's jackets, before I took them to the dry cleaners, sometimes smelled like perfume.

When we left, when we threw the party, we left the door open all night. After the last of the last of the people had kissed us on the cheeks, when they had gone, M closed the door and turned to me. As he turned, loose and expansive and happy, happy to be alone with me, he knocked an open bottle of red wine off the grange ermitage table we had by the door. It fell tumbling, arcing almost absurdly, almost slowly, into the beautiful wool rug. The wool of the carpet was so thick that the bottle didn't break, didn't even make a sound, just swallowed it all up and M and me, we just watched all the wine glug out onto it. Sloshing, gurgling, glugging, extravagant and monstrous, and grotesque, spreading for, well, for what seemed like a long time, across the wool. I wanted to tell my mother that now, sometimes I felt like the carpet, drinking things up, and not choosing what, and sometimes I felt like the bottle, caught and not breaking. That sometimes I felt like these things, the carpet and the bottle, rather than the owner of the carpet and the bottle, like I had been before.

At last M came back, late one night, from his trip. I smiled so wide when he opened the door and practically ran over to him to take his bags. He'd surprised me and I wished I'd been wearing something a little fresher, had done my hair maybe, or had cleaned the grit out from underneath my nails.

How was your trip? I said. How was work? What did you see? I was speaking too quickly I knew, showing by how much I talked how little I'd gotten to while he was away. I wished stupidly, for just a moment, to be wearing the same outfit that he was wearing, we could talk then I thought, if I were wearing wool pants and a button-up shirt with a pressed collar. If I were, I would have had something to say.

In the end it didn't matter. He was tired. He didn't want

to talk. He had a tan, a new haircut. Jesus he said, walking past me, walking over to open the windows in the living room. Look at this place. He was whispering, we both were. The children were asleep. Oh, I said, looking around.

We were only playing, I wanted to say to M. Or, really what I wanted to say was that I was having trouble sleeping here, in the apartment. Or, that I was having trouble being in this new place where I couldn't talk to anyone. That if I were honest, this wasn't what I'd been expecting. That sometimes my breath caught in my throat. But, in the end I only said, Oh, because I couldn't really say anything else. Because really, seeing the apartment as M must have seen it then, well maybe it did look a bit terrible.

I'd left up the fort that E had built for her animals in the living room, made out of sheets from the bed that M wanted now, to sleep on. I hadn't cleaned out the lemons from the day before and maybe there were flies. Really, I should have been prepared, should have been more ready to welcome him home. But I'd made some miscalculation. Wait, I said, cleaning up the fort, pulling the pillows off the kitchen floor without explaining why they were there, but wishing, really wishing that he would ask. I made the bed up while he sat down on the sofa. He seemed to really want to not talk and of course the kids were asleep. So I just got on with it and he started to get up to help me and I said, No, no really, sit down. You've been travelling all day, you must be exhausted.

After he went to sleep I wanted to fall into bed with him but I remembered the guest room and I didn't want him to find it in the morning and think, well, I don't know what. So I packed all the things I'd collected there into a garbage bag and took it all out to the bins and when the guest room was empty again I felt better about things. Better but also as if I were keeping secrets.

I sorted through M's laundry, separating the things that I could wash at home from the things that would need to be taken to the dry cleaners. I shook some sand out of the bottom of his pockets and swept all the grains up into a little pile on the floor. I put my finger on it for a moment, on the pile of sand, and pretended like a part of me, a tiny part, was somewhere else, on a beach.

Afterwards, I found I couldn't quite climb into bed with M, so I tried curling up beside B's crib on the sofa, but I couldn't sleep there either. Instead I took the broom and the rags and started to clean the kitchen, spraying and wiping all the surfaces. I cleaned out the drawer where I'd been stuffing the tram tickets. The salt and pepper shakers were shining now on the counter and the chairs were pushed into their places at the little kitchen table. I made it so it was as if no one lived in the apartment.

All the rental company's things were restored to their rightful places, just like in the pictures that I had looked at in the rental agency office. We were all being called back from somewhere else. I was. I felt certain that with everything brought back to just the way it had been before we'd come, that I would begin to sleep soon. That I would be allowed to. That the world would return to its place under my feet.

I practised saying the new names of things as I cleaned. Robinet. Balai. Compteur. Enfant. I was surprised to find that the night passed easily this way, when usually it was so long. I got out the knives even, to sharpen them, and I got out too the little stone that the rental company had left for that purpose. Scritch. It made such a wonderful noise! The knife on the stone, getting sharper and sharper and sharper. Crickets in the apartment, chirping, keeping me company, well, it sounded a bit like that. Like music! Scritch, scritch, scritch.

In the early early morning, I ran to the little store on the corner. I was there right when it opened. I grabbed eggs and coffee, bacon, bread, croissants, wild strawberry jam. I cooked breakfast, arranged the table, cups, bowls, plates, paper napkins folded under forks. Sparkling glasses placed just so, ready for juice. I felt so happy just then, in that moment, I felt that I could have cooked a thousand perfect breakfasts all at once.

M woke up, showered, and came and ate with B and E. He smiled at the way E brought her animals to the table and set them up in a ring around her plate, ready to watch her eat. He ran his fingers through B's silky puffs of hair. He also looked sometimes at me. We all smiled at each other.

Then M pushed away from the table. He put his plate and cutlery in the sink. I have to go to work, he said. Of course, I said. Have a good day, I said. I'll be back tonight, he said. I'll be back for dinner. OK, I said, that's great, and I felt at once a desire to cook the most wonderful thing, boeuf bourguignon maybe where you open up a bottle of wine and let the whole thing just slide into the pot, something extravagant, and exceptional and surprising, and I also wanted to empty all the pots onto the kitchen floor and shout at him, who will cook the dinner you're saying to me now that you're going to eat. Who will cook that. He kissed me on the cheek. He picked up his briefcase. He went to work. My mother always told me that happiness is a choice, only sometimes we have to hold to it very tight and keep choosing it.

Part Two

January

Visiting hours are two to four. That's what the sign says. The one that you're spraying and wiping. You can't see it now under the cloth but that's what it says. In case you didn't know. In case you sprayed and wiped without really looking. Which is quite understandable! But that's what it says: two to four: visiting hours.

What I'm wondering is, why is it posted in here? In here with me I mean. I'm not a visitor. Is it also posted outside? Anywhere outside? Can people outside, I mean to say visitors, can they see that sign? If they can't, how would they know when to come?

Could you pass me that cup of water? It's just, it's just that I'm very thirsty. And, I'd get it myself, but, well, I'm a bit tied up at the moment. Hah! Tied up, see?

In a minute? OK. Thank you.

It's just that my mouth gets so dry.

They're going to come and wash my hair today, cut it maybe. Good, I say. Good and great. Cut it all away. Shave it down to the skin.

They will be coming to my room to cut it. Makes me feel like a lady, you know? Having all these people come.

I hope you don't mind me talking. They told me I should. Talk, I mean. And I said, Well, what about?

And they said, like they do: Well, what about?

I yelled at them then, and I know now that I shouldn't have. That it's wrong and unhelpful. Unproductive. I know that. And they were right! They were right to do what they did. It's nothing that they shouldn't have done. Or do again if it needs doing.

I see all that now. The helpfulness of remaining still and quiet and good I mean. I see it!

But, just between you and me, sometimes, it's like I have a rock on my chest. A real one. An actual rock set right on top of the bone and it's crushing me. One of those big boulder things that you see sometimes by the ocean. Have you seen those? The ones

*that are so big and grey and you know if you licked them you
would taste salt? Anyway, what's important is that it's big, this
salty rock. You'd never be able to move it. Or I won't. Not ever.*

*And sometimes, also, the rock is inside me. There's this grit in
the back of my mouth. I can taste it, and I don't know whether
it's the grit of the rock, the rock inside me, or my own teeth
being ground into powder. It could be either one really. And
I'm right here between them. I'm here and there are these two
rocks pressing.*

*Yes. I'm sorry. No. I'm calm. You don't need to call anyone.
Really, you don't need to. I'm calm. What I meant to say is, it
just doesn't seem possible really, to talk to them. But to you,
well, I feel that I can. I hope that you don't mind that. It seems
better somehow, if we both have to be here together. It seems
better to fill the air up with something. Could we smoke? Do
you have a cigarette? I'm not particular, I'll smoke anything
at all.*

*No, I'm kidding. Yes, I understand. Who you are, who I am.
I understand that. I'm not trying to cross any lines! There are
boundaries, and boundaries are important! I understand that.
It's OK if you want to tell them what I tell you. I understand if
you need to. I just don't want to talk to them directly, you see?
Can you see that?*

We have so much time! Have you noticed that? There is so much time here! It's like it grows in the walls. Spawning and blooming and spreading and spawning and spawning and spawning. Like mould. The minutes ooze like spores across the surface of the day, slick, and orange and I've got this weight. Right on my chest. It's like a rock. Like an actual rock.

*   *   *

Do you like my hair? I can't see it. Not really. Only if I look in the window with my eyes half closed like this and only if the light is just right. But really, it feels amazing. The lady who came to wash it did such a wonderful job.

You should take care of yourself, she said to me, while she was brushing it. My old hair. She said that to me!

You know they tell me sometimes at appointments, when they're feeling kind, the doctors, I mean, they tell me, Slow down, breathe, imagine you are in the woods. Close your eyes, they say, and imagine you are walking in the woods. Imagine the ground you are walking on. Imagine that you are walking and you see two trees, the biggest ones, they say, that you have ever seen. Imagine that they are so big, these two trees, that you cannot see the tops of them, that their trunks disappear behind their branches. That they bury themselves, these two trees, deep into the chest of the sky. Like spears. Imagine the forest is a field of spears, spears that are tall enough and sharp enough to pierce absolutely all the things, all the things that you have ever . . .

No. I'm kidding. Of course it doesn't go like that. They do tell me the bit about the trees though. The two big ones. Only, they only ever ask me what I see when I step between them, the two big trees in the forest. That's what they want to know. But I never do, see it I mean. The forest. The two trees.

Only I did with her. With the lady who came to brush my hair. For a moment I could see them. The two big trees with a between between them, and a room there behind them.

I don't mean to keep you. I'm trying not to I promise! It's just that I've been thinking about something. She touched me, the lady who brushed my hair, after she was done. She touched me here, just behind my ear, with two of her fingers. What I mean to say is, well, it felt extra. Like she didn't have to. Like she didn't have to but she did. It's just that I've been thinking about that.

6

With M back, the days were made into hours again, into minutes. There was just enough time in the morning to run to the store and do the shopping while M and E and B slept. Just enough, if I did everything right and didn't take too long deciding.

If everything was done we could all sit for a moment together and smile at each other before M had to leave. Then cleaning. Washing, dusting, on my knees and pushing a damp rag into all the corners. Everything tidy and in its right place, even me.

I had to be quite severe with myself. To write rules and stick to them. To be firm so I wouldn't slip. After all, when you're falling who knows where you might end up. Things needed to always be done quickly and in the right order, laundry left in the dryer would wrinkle and become irretrievable, likewise groceries left out on the counter, likewise the dust, which if ever at all left to settle would invite in and collect more dust. I bought a bottle of linseed oil and began rubbing it into the wooden floor of the guest room, massaging the parquet with a little square of cloth, making it shine. The whole room seemed to glow when I was done. There were results, there was satisfaction. There was always more to do.

At night too, there was lying down next to M, right close up next to him, and there was the jumping up. Bam! Just like that, when B cried or E cried, and I was needed.

In the afternoon we still went to the park, but we had to leave early, packing up our things along with all the other busy mothers who had to get home to make dinner for their husbands. Who had to wash their children clean for bed. There was so much business and busyness. So much attending to. All the hours and hours and hours filled up by necessary things. Everyone was so purposeful. We were all so relieved to be occupied.

Nell didn't hurry to leave the park though, with me, with the other mothers. She was never brisk and bustling, clicking her tongue and checking her watch, she was never in a hurry to go at all, and I envied the way she lay there, on her picnic blanket, twined up and in between her baby and her son. I was envious but also a bit miserly with my tasks, protective of them. Of course, I could have lain down in the park right beside her and played with B. Go play, I could have said to E. We can stay all day. Sorry, I could have said to M when he got home, there's nothing to eat. Of course I could have.

Fine, he would have said, that's fine, but I didn't want him to. I didn't want him to say it, and I knew that he would. So I kept rushing home to cook, to have dinner ready and nice-looking, even though M never ate much of what I made.

M began to leave early anyway for work. Too early to make breakfast for him. Too early for us all to sit together at the little table in the kitchen. Things were difficult at work, things weren't going well. Or perhaps things were going very well. In either case, M was required earlier and earlier, and later and later too. More and more was needed of him. Or he felt he was needed. Or he told me he was. Everything was so unclear really and I felt too embarrassed to ask for clarification. I would lie down on his side of the bed after he left, my head where his head had been for just a moment.

I kept cooking dinner every night, even though I sometimes saw Nell in my head while I did it, while I cooked I mean, and wondered what she was getting up to, lying maybe in the sun all afternoon. I thought too sometimes of Aurelie, I thought of a kitchen filled with bouquets. A kitchen with no pots or dishes in it, only flowers.

I made sauces for pasta with tomatoes so ripe and heavy with juice that it seemed a mercy to slice them open, a relief to them. My knives were so sharp that they shivered through the skin of the tomatoes, or the eggplants or the berries or the grapes. I could have shaved my arm with them.

I made salads the way we liked with olive oil and large flakes of salt. We would wait for M in the apartment, sitting at the dinner table, ready and eager to see him. We would wait however long it took.

Well, Spanish people wouldn't think of eating dinner before ten o'clock. We could be so cheerful thinking of ourselves like that, E and B and I. We're becoming so European I would say to them and no one as the hours ticked past us. As the food became cold. It was always such a delight to have him home at night, to be the kind of family that ate dinner together, to be doing these important, these universally recommended things. I felt a lifting in my shoulders, somewhere just under the bones, a lightness, that carried me through the week. I didn't mind washing dishes at midnight. I didn't mind it a bit. I wondered if Nell washed dishes, if Aurelie did, I wondered how they felt if they did or if they didn't.

I began going out at night. Only when M was home. Only when he was asleep. I would say to myself, we need this or that, a sponge, or dish soap, even though I knew the corner store was long closed for the night. I would say perhaps, tonight, perhaps right now, it will be open. Or I would say, I'll take the garbage out. I would say it quietly, whispering, only talking I guess to myself, and to the apartment but still, I would say it, just to be saying something.

I would get dressed carefully when I left, put on a skirt maybe, or the heavy earrings that I had worn when I got married, something special, and instead of taking out the garbage or looking in the shop window at the sponges, I would go and sit in the cafe across the street and order a coffee and pretend that I smoked cigarettes.

Maybe I was going there because the old woman with the long purple coat was there too. I know you, I thought, and maybe I did. I could see the way she must pin her hair in front of the bathroom mirror in her apartment, the hook that she must hang her purple coat on, the drawer of rolled nylons in her dresser. Perhaps she knew me too, could see the rumpled pouch I kept my blush in, how all the powder was old and crumbly, how I wore it anyway, the blush, the skirt, the earrings, all of it, to sit alone in a cafe across the street from my apartment building, looking most of the time at the locked-up shutters of my living room.

But really probably, I was going there because once, through my window at night, when I'd been cleaning, I'd seen Nell walking past the cafe alone. At least I'd thought it was Nell. What I'd seen had been a woman alone that really could have been her, and she had hurried past the window, almost you could say stumbled past the window, and I had said, Oh, and put down my rag and spray and almost opened the window to say, Wait, let me, but of course she was already gone.

7

On Saturday M took us to look at the lake and to ride in the yellow boats that taxied people across. We all dressed as if for a picture. I put E in a white dress and braided her fine blonde hair, first one side, then the other. B was put in a blue romper and settled into his stroller. I smoothed his hair with a licked finger. I wore a dress that I'd brought with me, that I'd bought at the last minute, just before we left, when all of our things were gone or in boxes, and we'd sold the house.

Normally, I didn't wear dresses. This dress was a dress that I'd bought for someone else, a new person, a person that was not yet me. I bought it for a person living in some place I had never yet been, and yet here I was living in that place. I had yet to really become that new person I suppose because the dress caught me in the wrong places. It gathered me up, pinched me. Wearing it, I was turned this way and that on the end of its finger. I hesitated before I left the apartment.

I thought about changing into something different but B began to cry. There was no time.

The lake was beautiful, dotted with the white sails of boats manned by people who looked good in any kind of light, people who maybe didn't even need a boat to float across the water. People who packed champagne in picnic baskets and found it still cold when they were ready to drink it. E waved at these people from the side of the lake, some of the people on the boats waved back, everyone was so good-natured. M smiled at me, seeing E in her white dress by the lake all the way here in this different place, and we were just like that for a while, smiling and being smiled at.

We bought an ice cream for E, pink, two scoops piled high on top of a waffle cone. The lake was so clear that we could see the birds diving all the way to the bottom, scrabbling against the rocks on the lake bed with their bills. Their feet pumping underwater, we could see every bit of them. Nothing was a mystery to us.

There was so much sun. I knew that I would begin to sweat, knew that there was only minutes, perhaps seconds, before terrible stains would begin advancing across the fabric of the dress. The dress that was not proving after all to be for me. The treacherous stains would creep out from underneath my arms, they would stretch across my back.

We watched the other families, hand in hand like us. We smiled at sticky-cheeked children running along the white stones by the lake. We cooed at the strollers gliding by on all sorts of wheels. It got hotter and hotter. The heat was like a hand held tight over my mouth.

Women floated by all around me in billowing dresses. They looked serene, they looked like well-lit jellyfish. I needed not to be caught in the sun. I needed to find shade, ice, the dark inside of the apartment. M continued on ahead, running with E, pointing at the birds. A headache drifted across the bridge of my nose. We got in line to ride the boats. We would spend all day by the lake however we were.

Later, we had dinner at a pizza place in the old town. There were so many people crammed around the little tables, and into all the spaces between the little tables, that it was hard for the waiter to find us. We waited for a long time at the table, E colouring, M and me saying what a good job she did. How nice this was, and that.

When the waiter came M ordered a bottle of wine, a good one, from a region in Italy that we could now one day go to, that we were now living somewhat close to. We drank it knowing this and smiled at E and B and at each other. When a man came by the table holding a dozen or so plastic-wrapped roses, and asked M if he wanted to buy some 'for the beautiful ladies', M replied in perfect French that he would. That he definitely would, and bought them all. M and I laughed and piled the roses up high on our table in such a way that when our food came the plates had to be placed here and there among them. We laughed again and looked at each other and knew that we were lucky because here we were right in the middle of such a wonderful minute of our lives.

I'm not sure if the problem was that they had put a lot of spice in my pizza. I'm not sure if perhaps they had made me the wrong one, and M the right one, because we'd both ordered the same, the house special, but I found I could hardly eat without choking. Without my eyes burning, without tears coming out of my eyes and I kept laughing and wiping the tears on my napkin and drinking more wine. The more I tried to bite the pizza, though, the more impossible I found it even to bring it near my mouth. More and more there at the table, among the roses, the scent of the chillies seemed to find me, or the cheese, or whatever it was that was making me cry and sweat and dab at my face with my napkin until it was wet and ruined and to laugh and take E's napkin and make a who-knows face at M. Finally I just left the pizza where it was on the plate, almost untouched, the cheese going all cold and hard and ruined at the edges. Something wrong? M asked me, his plate was empty. Of course he'd loved it, of course it had been wonderful, and perfect, and really I felt stupid and entirely unable to say.

When we walked back to the tram stop we filled B's stroller with the roses. I carried B soft and sleeping in my arms. E ran alongside and M pushed the stroller and people looked up from their tinkling tables and smiled at us as people do when everything is wonderful, when everyone has found a shade of lipstick they are really pleased with and the moments seem to be already photographed, already cut up into instants and tucked away for later, for looking at and showing. When we got back to the apartment E and B went straight into their beds and M and I unwrapped the roses and piled them into the vase and gave them water.

I had drunk more wine than I realized and of course, I had eaten less than I meant to, and I began to feel it now. The alcohol buzzing and humming me along as if I stood on a boat's deck. I slipped a little. M put his hand on my back, I leaned into him and kissed his neck, and suddenly I couldn't tell if these things were choreographed. The way I pressed against him, the way I slipped a shoulder out of my dress. We had done these things so many times before that it was hard to tell. Want versus habit, desire versus something else, routine maybe. My fingers here, and his here.

He kisses me twice here and I kiss him back. One. He puts his arms around me. Two. He leans in to drop his lips to my neck. Three. Now we would move to the bed. M would suggest this. Should we move to the bed? he would say. And we would leave the kitchen and I would slip the other shoulder out of my dress, my dress that I'd been longing to get out of anyway, and it would fall to the floor and we would fall onto the bed and quietly try to find something of each other there. To make of it what we could without waking E, B, the neighbours. Even in this, we had to be careful, composed. There was even now, a certain right way to proceed.

Instead, M stopped, lifting his fingers, his lips, from my skin so suddenly that I shivered, felt cold. I have something for you, a surprise, he said. My eyes must have gotten wide, maybe I looked suddenly greedy because he laughed a little to make it casual. It's nothing really, he said, just something I picked up for you in Rome, while I was away. And, well, I meant to give it to you when I got back, but, he hesitated, trailed off. Looked at me.

But what, I said, starting to feel, well, a sharpening. A turning or a descent maybe. The conversation shifting. Suddenly I didn't like M looking at me.

It's just, he said, hesitating again, drawing the words out, making everything take a long time. What happened tonight, he said, at the restaurant.

It wasn't a question.

And when I got back, he said. From the trip, I mean, I don't know, he said.

Ask me to go to bed I thought, right now, feeling hotter and hotter, wishing the conversation would swing away from wherever it was going. Why were we still standing in the kitchen. Ask me to go to bed, I said urgently without moving, without moving my lips.

Something was off wasn't it, M said. When I got back, I could feel it. There was something about the air in the apartment, it was so, I don't know, so stale. What happened, he asked, while I was gone?

I took a breath and refused absolutely to remember any details about the way my hands shook during those days, about the feeling of flying and falling at the same time inside the apartment, about being unable to brush my teeth. Take me to bed I wanted to scream at him.

When I didn't answer, M said, Sorry. I don't know what I was thinking. He hugged me and kissed me on the shoulder and slipped the strap of my dress back up onto it. Anyway he said, about the present. Wait a second, he said, leaving me in the kitchen, spinning, trying to catch my breath.

M came back holding a long trench coat draped in his arms like a fainted woman or a bride. It was beautiful, soft camel, wide lapels. A double row of buttons just itching to be touched, to be done up, to be undone. The coat's waist would touch exactly my waist.

My ankle slipped beneath me when I saw it. It was that much. With a coat like that around me, I could have been anyone underneath. It was a thing of myth. If I had been an armful of hay it could have spun me into gold. I almost fell but caught myself on the counter. For a moment the glass vase and I occupied exactly the same space, for a moment I was eye to eye with all the roses and it was unclear which one of us would fall. I recovered though and the vase slipped off the counter and smashed into a thousand pieces on the floor. Water, roses, glass. A tiny flood. The little glass shards worming themselves into every corner of the kitchen as quick as that. Shards that could creep into E's feet, B's hands, all their tender so soft skin.

M left with the coat, to hang it up somewhere, and I dropped to my knees, sweeping, cleaning, wiping. Care had to be taken. M helped a bit and then went to bed, saying something about work in the morning. Saying, stop cleaning, it's fine. Saying stop. Saying come to bed. I stayed in the kitchen, I needed to be sure everything was clean, ordered. When I was done I peeled off my dress, finally, finally, and threw it into the garbage bag with the glass, the roses. The expensive fabric floated in the bag for a moment rippling like moonlight on dark water, just pouring itself out under the black plastic sky, the glittering chipped glass stars.

I cinched the ties around it all and knotted the bag tight. I slipped on an old T-shirt and sweats and pushed my feet into the lovely leather loafers that M wore to work. I grabbed the bag and headed out to the bins. It was better to have it all over and done with, put away, disposed of, to wake up to a morning in the apartment with no evidence of any day before.

On my way to the bins I passed the sign forbidding the disposal of garbage after nine o'clock, stepping softly on the thick soles of M's beautiful shoes. I pushed open the top of the garbage bin and threw the bag down inside. It was amazing how still everything was. The big concrete buildings all around me were filled with families. Kids, dogs, cats, washing machines, all different kinds of lives stuffed into one, two, three bedroom boxes, and yet after ten o'clock everyone was quiet in exactly the same way. Just the way, I thought, that everyone either was or would be dead in the same way too. When we're quiet we're dead! I might have yelled, but didn't.

There was a rustling behind me and I spun around. Over on the far side of the bins, by the paper recycling, crouched the woman from the cafe. She was squatting in a pile of garbage, opening boxes, running her fingers inside them. She pulled a crust from a wet-looking pizza box and began to eat it with one hand while she continued to search through more boxes with the other. A box of matches fell out of her sleeve and she snatched it back up again and dropped it into the pocket of her coat. She pulled pieces of what must have been some kind of sandwich from a small box lying on the ground, these too she shoved into her pockets. She finished the pizza crust and began chipping something off one of the other boxes, dried cheese maybe. She licked her fingers, ran her fingernails along her gums. Her eyes shot up to meet mine and she smiled at me, a finger still in her mouth. I could smell her breath, the things caught between her teeth, the damp rottenness of her gums. I felt gutted. Rooted and gutted and gasping.

I stumbled back and crashed into the garbage bin behind me. The noise was like snow cracking in the Alps. An avalanche. A noise that promised casualties. A light flicked on in an apartment above us. If I was seen, I could be reported, denounced. I jumped sideways into the shadowed grass, onto the carefully tended grass where it was forbidden to go. There was a sign posted by the concierge, promising terrible things to those that stepped off the concrete. One of M's beautiful loafers sank into a pile of fresh dog shit.

I ran across the lawn that was not to be run across. When I reached the safety of the covered concrete walkway that led back to the apartment I looked back and saw the woman in the purple coat watching me. Light from the street spilled onto her, pooling in the folds of her coat, she hadn't moved and as I watched she pulled another crust out of a box and began eating it. I ran back to the apartment and locked the door, stopped my ragged breathing in my throat. I would have to tell the rental company about the vase.

8

M was gone when I woke up. I had slept like a wall had been pulled down on top of me. Slept like I'd never not slept. I woke up and was a different person, someone who was definitely capable of moving through the day, of taking care of B and E, of sitting by the pump for hours smiling happily, of never wanting for any amount of time even for a single second to run away screaming from wherever I was, whatever I was doing. I had slept all night in the same bed as M. I wondered if we had touched, if we had drifted toward each other in some hour or other, if he had put his leg over mine, or me his. Surely such a thing was possible.

There was a note beside me on the side table but the ink was smudged. Be back late, it might have said. Or, I love you the same as always no matter what. Shoes? it might have said. WTF? it might have said. It could have easily said that. I could have called him and asked him, only he would be in meetings all day, and I hated to interrupt. Also, I had ruined his shoes. Of course I had, and the day, the real day as it would be and not my imagining of it, began to settle down on top of me like some great bird landing on my shoulders with all its unnatural weight.

The apartment smelled of dog shit. I opened the window in the living room and saw the concierge scrubbing at a line of brown stains, footprints on the concrete walk. He had hauled out steaming water, buckets of rags, telescopic mop handles and scrubbers of various sizes, the works. The footsteps as he cleaned them would lead, I knew, down the walk and into the building and straight to the door of the apartment. There would be no denying anything.

I wouldn't be able to leave. We would have to hide all day inside where we could never be found. I almost couldn't breathe, the smell was really horrendous, seeping into all the fibres and fabrics, the sheets, the curtains. How had I forgotten about it all while I'd slept?

Perhaps it was possible to construct a new world out of a smaller space, a whole world out of less. Perhaps it was possible to create a world that was less connected to other things. To make the apartment into a meteor: fast moving and unassailable. I lowered the aluminium shutters and shut out the concierge. Winked him out as fast as blinking.

The apartment was dark now, but cosy. A cave for us. We could play bears all morning. E would love it, we could have so many good hours like that, growling at each other, pawing at the rental-company sofa with our so big paws. I could smile so wide when we played, wide like I might tear my face at the corners and show the whites of my eyes and it would be OK because it would be part of a game. When E got tired of being a bear I would shout, Now we are underwater, now we are secret underwater things.

There were bananas for breakfast, just turning brown, milk. I made coffee and worked on my French exercises while I waited for B and E to wake up. Sleep filled the apartment like a magic spell. Soft breathing, the sweat of dreaming babies. Perhaps a wall of roses would spring up and protect me from the concierge. Perhaps there would never be a knock at the door. Perhaps we could stay here in this apartment and sleep for a hundred years. Perhaps we would never be unhappy. Malheur. Malheureux. Malheureuse.

I went to the bathroom to take a shower, leaving my coffee only half drunk on the table. This was of course a dangerous thing, a terrible thing, for a mother to do. A hot drink on the table, steam curling like a snake, tempting tempting little just-woken hands to grab it. I left it anyway, feeling already penitent. Already explaining myself to someone, the police maybe. I was often, almost always really, explaining myself to the police in this hypothetical way. Practising for disaster, for post-disaster, for the moment after, I guessed. Imagining my words, my hysteria. I had just stepped away for a moment! I would say, and I would be feeling like I did now, when I said it, with the panic rising in my chest, slipping its fingers between my ribs and cracking them open, or perhaps I would just be screaming when they tried to ask me. Perhaps I would be standing alone behind a wall of noise.

In the bathroom there was a mess of packets on the counter. A bottle of pills stood half open, painkillers that a pharmacist had prescribed to me for headaches. Packets of vitamin powder were spilled haphazardly in the sink. Several of the little foil and plastic squares that held M's pink allergy pills were ripped open. The mirrored door of the medicine cabinet swung on its hinges. Bottles of shampoo lay on their sides, everything dripped. Everything was in disarray.

E? Had E done this? I should rush to her room, and wake her, take her temperature, make sure she hadn't taken any pills, make sure she wasn't now not sleeping, but drifting in some kind of drug-induced fever, unable to get up. I hesitated, waking a child was irrevocable. It could be nothing, the apartment was so quiet with the children asleep. I was in the bottom of a ship, I could have been all alone.

I crept once, when I was a girl, in the middle of the night into my parents' bedroom and opened up my mother's dressing-table drawer which, to me at the time, seemed like the secret key to everything about her. The drawer was filled with her tubes and bottles, her tiny glass jars. I loved to watch her take a dab of one thing, a pinch of something else. I loved to watch her looking at her own face in the mirror, making it, as I watched, beautiful. It was like when the peel falls from the apple whole, without breaking, her true face emerged like that.

87

In the dark that night, that night that I was sneaking, I pulled open her drawer and grabbed a handful of tubes and tubs and bottles, all small things of various shapes. I meant to take them back to my room and examine them. Out in the hall though, I slipped and fell and the bottles crashed to the floor and spilled everywhere. When I got up I was standing on a handful of sharp little things. I made it back to my room and switched on my desk lamp and found several baby teeth stuck to the bottom of my foot. Afterwards I had a very particular horror of stepping on things and insisted on wearing slippers always in the dark, even under the covers of my bed. Children can be strange for all sorts of reasons.

E wasn't tall enough to make a mess like this though, she couldn't possibly reach up into the medicine cabinet or reach high enough to have been the one to have written with the lipstick on the walls up near the ceiling. It was my name anyway, that was written up there on the wall. It really was! And E couldn't spell. Perhaps M had left for work in a rush. Perhaps he had been feeling unwell. Perhaps he had been upset. I cleaned the bathroom. Returned it to order, screwing the caps on the bottles, wiping down the sink, the faucet, scrubbing until everything was perfect. Standing on the toilet I could just reach the lipstick writing and wipe it away but it was quite hard and I almost lost my balance several times.

There were two trees that stood in a field across the street from the apartment I lived in with my mother. When the rains came as they often did, and clouds hung like a heavy grey ocean over the field it looked to me like the clouds, the ocean-clouds hung directly above these two trees, as if they, poor scraggly things, were the anchor for the whole world. It looked also, when the rains came, as if they, the trees, were about to be destroyed. The birds that lived in the field would fly to the trees and beat their wings just before the rain fell and their wings, then, as the colour drained from the field and everything grew dark, would look like black leaves shining, wet and slick and glinting in the last shreds of light.

The reason I loved and hated to watch them though, the birds, was that they could never decide which tree to shelter in, the one on the left or the one on the right. They could never decide which of the two would save them. Because it was plain that they knew, the birds, that one, but only one, would. They would settle in one tree, calling to each other, screaming almost as the winds came, and then one would leave, make the desperate flight to the other tree, and all the others, screaming, would follow. Perhaps I thought so often of these trees because my mind felt like this now that I had children, my thoughts so often screaming and beating their wings, flying uselessly from one tree to the next. Should I be worried now about the coffee cup or the pills? Was there some other thing I couldn't see? Some disaster that I could not now imagine? The only safety, the only shelter, seemed to be to stay in the air, in constant flight.

I took a shower. Steam filled the little room, beading on the sink, the mirror. I let the water run over my skin until it began to lose its heat. I dried myself slowly, obstinately taking my time. I wrapped my hair in a towel and opened the bathroom door. B was crying in his crib, E was calling for me.

After lunch we escaped out the window to the little park. I couldn't face the front door, the concierge, the freshly scrubbed walk, the garbage bins. None of it. The surfaces would be clean now of course of footprints, of fingerprints, of breath. Restored, and I didn't want to see them restored. I didn't want to see it cleaned up somehow, what I had done. Besides, it was quicker to go to the park through the window, more direct. If we went through the window we could be there so much faster, there, in the park where we could love each other and play.

So when we left, we slid out of the apartment through the back window and dropped down to the soft green grass that wasn't ours, that was on the wrong side of the little fence. We're so fast! I said to E, to make her run across the grass. Look at us! I said to her, holding her hand, holding B in my other arm, his soft little baby head pressed to my chest. No one can catch us! We're birds, we're flying!

Well we were a bit like birds just then I suppose, the way they hop hop hop before they fly. Anyway I tried to make it into a game. The game of course being designed to make her hurry, to make her just the right amount of afraid. The fox will eat the baby birds who fall behind, I told her while we streaked across the lawn. The greedy greedy fox will gobble them up.

When we got to the park, I set B down on our blanket and gave him a toy to play with. I settled E with her tools, her pail, and listened to her list of endless duties regarding the proper care of her animals. The baby giraffe was feeling poorly. E seemed pleased to announce this. She flew off to bury it neck-deep in sand. A treatment, she said.

The mother giraffe will be worried, I said. Take her too. E refused and this hurt me somehow. Smiling, I took the mother giraffe to the edge of the sandbox and set her down next to the baby. There, I said, now she can watch. E moved her game to the other side of the sandbox leaving the mother giraffe staring out at nothing, balanced on her spindly plastic legs. It bothered me, really bothered me, to see her like that. I even felt for a moment as if my own eyes were made of paint, as if I were trying desperately to see past a thick smear of acrylic, move legs that would never move, as if my baby might depend on me doing this impossible thing. It was a horrible feeling. E buried the baby, covering its head with a final shovelful of sand. It would almost certainly be lost.

Rain clouds had been gathering even as the heat rose and now the sky crackled with the coming storm. The other women had already gathered their children, calling to them in long and lovely strings of words that I could never hope to follow, and left the park, heading back to their unimaginable homes. On y va. On y va. À la maison.

All except Nell. She wasn't leaving. She lay on her back on her blanket playing with her baby, kissing his fingers, stopping to whisper in the older boy's ear. The blanket is a ship, perhaps she said, or maybe, the blanket can fly. We can make this happen if we lie here still together and never leave this one place that we are right now. Perhaps she whispered things like that to him. I had been determined to stay as long as she did, but I saw now that she had no intention of leaving, even as great fat drops of rain began to fall, dotting the sandbox, staining the front of her dress. I didn't know the word for lightning, couldn't make light of the weather, couldn't ask her why she wasn't leaving.

I called to E to come, to come now. I gathered B, who was beginning to cry, grabbed the blanket. The clouds opened. There would be lightning and plenty of it. E screamed and I pushed her forward, back to our apartment, the still open window, tripping, barely catching myself, B in my arms, all of our things in my arms too. Running away was such an awkward business.

Back in the apartment I dried E's hair, B's. Unpacked our wet things, hung the towel up to dry. When I looked back through the window to the park, Nell was still there with her children. They were lying on their backs in the rain.

An hour later, when I looked again, I saw a man standing over them with an umbrella, it looked as if he were yelling at her. He pulled her to her feet, really pulled her. He took the baby. He could have been yelling, she could have been, the rain would have covered up any sound. She could have been screaming and I wouldn't have heard it. I didn't think she was screaming. When I looked again they were gone.

After the rain stopped we discovered that the mother giraffe had been left at the park, but when I ran back to get her, I found the sandbox empty, only sticks and rocks and wet sand. E was sad when I told her this, but not overly so. The treatment had, after all, worked. The baby had been cured.

There was a woman's shoe lying beside the sandbox, an expensive looking ballet flat. It occurred to me that Nell must have lost her shoe, that she must have stumbled home in the rain with one bare foot. There was nothing to do of course but leave it there. Nothing to do but hope that she was fine and would eventually come and find it. When I jumped back through the window I lowered the shutters so I couldn't see out onto the little park anymore. It seemed better that way, safer. I had never had a man pull my arm the way that man had pulled Nell's, never in my life. Thinking of it made my skin sting in the places where he had touched her.

We couldn't go outside that afternoon, I couldn't, though E wanted to go to the store for ice cream. So I prepared the last of what was in the fridge for dinner. A fish I'd bought at the market, tomatoes, more lemons, more heat and flies and sugar. I cut the fish into pieces and pounded them into the wooden rental-company cutting board. When I picked up the pieces they were still studded with scales, scales that would, if she ate the fish, catch in E's teeth, that would make her cry, that would cause her real pain, that would stick sharply in her gums and her teeth. I watched it all fry in the pan, the scales, the smashed pieces of fish. The oil speckled my wrists like teeth, while the fish crisped, then hardened into a burnt shell, and the pan became a wasteland strewn with glistening scales, as if the fish had, after death, grown a thousand eyes. We waited for M but he didn't come. I threw the ruined, blackened fish away and E and I had crackers and cheese and tomatoes for dinner and we all three slept together, exhausted, in the same bed. I saw the coat hanging on M's side of the closet before I fell asleep, it was as beautiful as I remembered. In the morning I found a rumpled suit in a pile beside the bed, as if M had collapsed there. As if he'd become suddenly so exhausted that he'd fallen out of his clothes and disappeared.

February

I think about you all the time. All the time I do. I think about you and I think about Wait and I think about Let Me Explain, and then I think again about you and then I think again about Wait and then I think again about Let Me Explain. Like that.

Can I tell you about the woman who sleeps in here with me? In the bed under the window? I'm so glad we have a window. Any day there could be a bird. And really it's the windows that are important. Don't you think? For houses? Without a window, well you could be anywhere.

Anyway, I wanted her bed when I got here but they wouldn't let me take it. They said no. I asked why but they just said no.

That was before I understood. Or maybe that was the moment when I was beginning to understand. Understand, I mean, what kind of place here was. What kind of house. How I wasn't owed an explanation. And I see that now, the purpose of that. Of the saying No. But, back then, back before I understood what I understand, when they said No, I said What, like this: What??! and screamed and yelled a bit and I see now why they did what they did when I did that. I want you to know that I know that. That I see it clearly.

Are you telling them what I'm telling you? Well, if you are, you can tell them that I know and see that now.

Oh. Could you not clean under there? Under the bed? Please don't look under there. I'd feel so grateful. I really would. You don't have to worry. There's nothing there. It's not like that. There's nothing under the bed.

It's just that I would feel better if I knew there was some place in here, in this room, in this place, if I knew that there was some place where nobody but me ever looked. Ever. And see? It could be under the bed. The place. The private place. It could be there because, see? It's already dark.

You're always here so early in the morning. I see you come in because I'm awake early always too, even though I'm supposed to be practising staying in bed and breathing deeply and going back to sleep and not jumping up and running about when I wake up. I'm not though, practising. So, in the mornings, when the door at the end of the hall goes beep and clangs open and

you walk in, well I'm always already watching. From in here
I mean, with my face pressed up tight against the little plastic
window in the door.

It's the dreams. Once I'm awake, I'm so relieved to have
escaped them that, well, it makes no sense to lie down again
and try to sleep. Lord, lead us not into temptation!

My grandmother would say that before we ate Christmas
dinner. That was the last little bit of grace. Lord, lead us not
into temptation! And I could see it, sitting in my faux velvet
dresses that were a different colour every year but always
otherwise the same and my hair pulled into braids. I mean
I could see temptation, like a gingerbread house all done up in
icing and gumdrops. I could taste it in my mouth, temptation,
and I would know, with my guts turning to ice and concrete,
that I was already there, inside it, inside temptation. And I
would think, how do you get out when you're already there?
Well, you can understand how my grandmother never liked
having me for Christmas and would say over me to my
mother, I don't know why I ask you two. I cook all day and no
one eats.

But I meant to talk to you about the woman in the bed under
the window. The bed that was empty when I came here and
isn't now. Well, it's empty now obviously. She has an
appointment, but you know what I mean. What I mean to say

is, she snores! What can they be giving her that she sleeps like that? Could you ask for someone to change it? Because she snores and I can't wake her to tell her to stop.

I leapt up on her bed last night when I finally couldn't stand it anymore and screamed, There's a fire! There's a bloody fire and we'll all die in here if you don't wake up! But they only came and scooped me off her and gave me medicine and new appointments. But, don't you see? It was just the snoring!

So if you could tell them that, I would appreciate it, because I'd really rather not have any new appointments. And I can't take medicine that will trap me in my dreams. I have to be able to wake up. I have to know that I'll be able to wake up, or I'll never sleep. Never! And I'll begin to spin round and round like water going down a drain, and then, I'll be gone. Gone! Like the dodo! No, I'm all right, please don't go, you don't have to call anyone, really. See? I'll sit still like a lady.

I know it's not for me to say, I know that, but really, it was, last night I mean, it was really just because of the snoring.

9

Today M needed his beautiful suits to be beautifully clean. I wanted to be helpful, I had my purple dry-cleaning zip-bag. We could make a day of it. If every minute went just right I could clean the apartment, drop off the suits, stop by the market for the dinner things and spend the afternoon beside the pump. Every minute was a card and I could build the most beautiful house out of the day. I could buy raspberries at the market and eat them with E while B napped, we could carve out little secrets together like that if we were careful. Little secrets could be ways to love each other. I drank two or three glasses of wine every day at five o'clock. Little secrets could be ways, too, to love myself.

M wouldn't be back for dinner, he had said this crawling into bed, latelatelate the night before, smelling of red wine, maybe cigarettes. Or maybe I just imagined that he did. Maybe I hoped he did have dinner somewhere nice, a steak, a glass of wine, leaning back in his chair discussing something important with other important people, people who would understand important things. Or discussing something unimportant, laughing, and that being a break, a much needed break, from thinking about and discussing important things. How could I have not hoped for this?

He couldn't come home for dinner at all anymore, not for a little while. He said this, his hand finding my shoulder in the bed in the dark, his finger brushing over the small place where there was just the thinnest layer of skin over bone, and moving on, wanting something, a pillow maybe. We were sometimes like this, waymarkers, even if just a shoulder, weren't we? Wasn't that what we had, after all, promised always to be for each other?

Anyway he couldn't come, he was needed for interviews, meetings, drinks after work. Water beading along the side of a cocktail glass set on a table overlooking the lake. Ice-cold martinis, highballs, glasses clinking together, business cards, beautiful suits.

So we would not need to wait for M in the evenings and E and I could eat cream and melon and crackers if we wanted to. When M came home, whenever he came home, we would all be there breathing the same air. I drifted back into my half-sleep, waking, turning, slipping the other nipple into B's mouth. Sleep was like a dragonfly in my hands, always fluttering, always trying to get away from me.

My mother had terrible insomnia when I was growing up, she would go through periods of not sleeping so profound that she would begin to hallucinate, the edges of the house beginning to fall away, what was left beginning to bend around her. Not sleeping could be like that, could take you away, remove you to a place over which you had no control. The approaching night became a terror, so many hours to be alone in the dark. She tried various treatments but the one that I remember was the smiling therapy. She liked it, my mother, she thought it worked, and so for years she practised it, the therapy, in the evenings. The idea is to smile, even though you are afraid, or tired, or beginning to see the corners of the ceiling fill with bats, to smile continuously for minutes, for many of them, at various times throughout the day but especially at night. I remember finding her sitting still by herself with her mouth pulled into a wide grin, or cooking us dinner and smiling and smiling without stopping even though I could see that she was afraid. I tried this now sometimes at night, the smiling for many minutes, I imagined my teeth were like the bright phosphorescent things that float on the surface of the ocean at night. I imagined that and other things. The nights were so long sometimes. It would be good if M could make it home before too many hours had passed.

We went to drop off the clothes at the dry cleaners. It really wasn't very far to walk. It really was very far for us. B in his stroller, E walking beside me. We have to do this for Daddy, I said. E brought her giraffe and we passed through the front door of the apartment which was beginning to feel to me more and more like a portal, a barrier that separated two different kinds of real, something that could not always be depended upon to open, to be openable. I had begun feeling a bit like a crab leaving its shell when I stepped out the door. I began to feel like that even though I knew the thought was silly and wrong and not right. I balanced the purple zip-bag over the handles of B's stroller and we tried to pass for everyday people on the street. People who made sense here on this sidewalk in this particular part of the world. I tried to walk like a woman who could be spoken to.

Sometimes, walking like this, slowly, in the middle of the morning, behind and with and in between all the other women who were also pushing strollers, who also were carrying zip-bags for the dry cleaners and shopping lists in their pockets, it seemed that we were all ghosts, in the way that we were pale, yes, and in the way we lurched and glided, but also in the way that we were remnants, in the way we were unable to recall what had come before. Ghosts of business women or doctors or ghosts of shop clerks or teachers, and of course all of us were ghosts of little girls.

We passed the cafe. It was OK that we walked slowly. We had the whole day to do this one thing. It was OK and I could be an excellent mother who does not yell, Hurry up! Hurry up! Hurry up! to her child in a shrill ugly voice. We could smile and walk so slowly and that was fine and wonderful and of course we could stop and look at this flower and that flower and talk about them along the way. Of course we could do all this happily and slowly, of course we could take our time.

At the dry cleaners I presented my purple bag at the counter and duly received my receipts. There was a woman ironing, a mountain of shirts piled up beside her. It would take her all day to finish. I was so jealous. I really was! She was so good at what she did and she could do it all day in peace without stopping once.

Back at the apartment, E fed her giraffe sesame seeds. I fanned myself, changed my shirt, swatted at the flies, began to cut up something or other for lunch.

When we went to the park that afternoon Nell wasn't there. Her shoe wasn't there either. The shoe, at least, that I thought was hers. Perhaps she'd already come for it, or the man had, or someone had thrown it away. I felt restless all afternoon sitting there, filling a pail with water for B, dipping his fingers in it. Waiting for something to happen. Sometimes it seemed like being a good mother, the best, meant mostly covering yourself over in a layer of smiling and smiling. There was nothing to think about except making everything exactly right in the minute you were in. An endless happy present, dipping fingers in the water, see? Wet. Water. Cucumbers and crustless sandwiches, all that happiness built on the backs of a thousand tiny things.

The afternoon slipped away and we climbed back through the window into the apartment. I put B and E to bed and went into the guest room to oil the floor. I ran a wet towel over the plant to keep the dust off and pictured the room as it would be when it was perfect. I pictured myself just standing there inside it.

I was there for a long time, crouched in the small room that really could have been a closet except for the sink. Maybe I slept, when I left anyway, it was the middle of the night. M wasn't home. I switched off the light in the guest room and pulled the door closed. The apartment felt heavy in the dark, felt draped around my shoulders. I ran my finger along the counter in the kitchen, making sure that everything was clean, presentable, ready for the next day.

There was a noise at the door. A light scratching. Perhaps M had forgotten his keys. A thud hit the outside of the door. I heard a slithering, like fabric on the floor, then a tap, tap, like a finger, testing. It was almost hesitant, the sound. Tap, tap, tap, anybody home? I felt cold. Suddenly really cold and I could hear the blood start to hum in my ears, the stutter-whoosh of my heart.

I went to the door. I thought I wouldn't. I thought I might just fall to the floor in the kitchen and wait for it to be M, wait for him to walk through the door and find me. But it wasn't M. I walked to the door and pressed my cheek against it. I pressed my cheek up close to the wood but wasn't able to make myself look through the peephole. My heart really was beating so fast and my head was beginning to buzz, blood rushing in, rushing out. Here I was in the quiet so quiet midnight dark alone. This was the thing that would happen. The terrible thing.

The sounds drifted away but I stood there with my cheek to the door, with my hand on the handle for a long time, until light began poking through the metal storm shutters in the kitchen window. I stood there that long, though it was possible that I drifted in and out of sleep.

In the morning I felt stupid, finding myself standing there at the door. Believing something, being afraid of it. Thank goodness for morning and things to do. Dawn washes away so many ridiculous things, all suds and soap bubbles and light.

M had been away all night and hadn't told me. He hadn't come back for even a moment or I would have known it, standing like that, right behind the door. He hadn't crawled into bed with me and I hadn't been in bed. It felt like we had gone over something, M and me, without talking at all about it. It felt like some line or barrier had been crossed.

I made coffee and drank it standing by the small table in the kitchen, holding my eye right up to the shuttered window, peeking out between the slats. When E woke and wanted to roll the shades up, I would tell her no. I would tell her that today we were inside a submarine. That today was a day for pressing our eyes to peepholes and being silent like jellyfish or eels, a day for secrets, and double-hinging jaws. I would tell her something like that, when she got up. I set the table for breakfast in the wavy underwater light. In the corners of my eyes, I could see the kitchen begin to fill with sea creatures.

They hung up by the ceiling pulsing and expectant, like extravagant plants.

B woke and I fed him on the sofa in his pyjamas, his feet kicking at my arms, his fingers opening and closing in that particular baby way. I tried to count how many days old he was, how many hours, how many minutes. We fell asleep I guess, or, we fell into some space together that wasn't really awake, because when the door opened we both jumped. M walked into the room, wearing yesterday's suit, scattering the jellyfish, the anemones, the watery squid from their coves, their hiding places, their cosy seaweed nests, scattering also the soft knocks and taps, the shadow steps, the whisperings and knockings that had been gathering and gathering in the apartment while I sat alone with B and closed my eyes. He'd taken his shoes off at the door so he stood in the living room in his socks, showing me his knobbly, getting-older feet.

There you are, he said, as if we were the ones who had gone somewhere. He came over and put his fingers in B's hair and sat down next to me and put his arm around me, around us, around B and me both and leaned his head back against the wall and closed his eyes. E woke up and came into the room in her nightgown and I was pleased to have her find us like this. The picture was just right. We both smiled at her in just the right way. B even cooed or made some soft baby sound that was fitting. E rubbed her eyes, blinked and came to curl up between us. Being touched and seen and so familiar with each other, well, it felt then like everything would just go on and be absolutely beautiful for ever. Sometimes everything can seem right with your life if you pretend to take a picture of yourself at the perfect moment. Here we were.

M sighed and stretched, cracked his neck. I can't stay, he said. I've got to get back to work. I can't believe I didn't make it home last night.

We all tumbled off the couch and back into ourselves. I ran to the kitchen to boil water for more coffee, hoping that the beans were still fresh. Hoping that they were the kind of beans he liked. E needed breakfast too.

I need you to get something for me, M said. Already in a clean suit, already almost out the door before the water had boiled. My hands were shaking, I was trying to make his coffee that fast, scooping the grounds into the French press. Really I was thinking if I could only keep him for just a moment longer in the apartment everything would be better, would be right. Really I was also thinking of what I must look like, my hair flat, an old sweater thrown around my shoulders. Is that for me? M said. Looking at the French press, at the white mug with the blue flowers that I'd placed perfectly and rightly beside it.

Thanks, he said, but it's OK. My assistant can get it for me at work. He said a name but I didn't catch it. Some name that was like a kind of silk ribbon or a deer, long legs, eyes and eyelashes. His assistant.

Once a woman has had children she always looks like a woman who has had children. She looks like a woman who has always had children too and this is of course even worse. The coffee was so close to being almost ready. Wait, I said.

Sorry, he said, I really need to get going. I've got a meeting, he said and he rolled his eyes and made a mock-bored face. You know how it goes, he said, but of course I didn't, know I mean.

I need you to get something for me though, OK? he said. A baby gift, from us, something nice. Jean's wife just had a baby. Besides, he said, it will be good for you to get out of the apartment for a while. Get some fresh air. Do a little shopping. Maybe you'll see something nice for yourself, he said, smiling, offering, giving, what? Maybe I would.

Jean invited us over, to meet the baby, M said. We'll swing by his apartment this weekend, it's right on the lake! You'll love it. But we need a gift. You should get to know Polina, he said, dipping his head into the kitchen, coming for a second close to me. He smelled like soap and toothpaste. He smelled so good. You guys could get together, hang out, he said. You must need someone to talk to, he said, cooped up here alone all day.

I need you, I need you here to help me, I said. I need you here with me in this apartment, I need you here at night. But he couldn't hear me. He couldn't hear me because I didn't want him to hear me and I was saying all that into the empty coffee cup, muttering. M wasn't speaking quietly, his words swarmed up the walls and over me, charging, and taking charge. Black ink and capital letters. Sorry, what's that? he said, but his phone rang and he had to go. I had to go too. B was crying. I'd left him alone in his crib by the sofa in my hurry to make M coffee. E had hurt her toe pulling out a chair at the table. She was pulling on my shirt, needed ice, needed looking after.

Talking on the phone, M kissed me on the cheek and left, see you tonight, he said. I'll probably be back late. Love you guys.

I knew that he felt lucky that he had me to watch over E, to take care of B. I knew that he felt that what I was doing was difficult and important. Indispensable.

The door closed behind him. I dumped the boiling coffee down the sink and the pipe steamed and gurgled and belched out a rotting smell and for a moment I just stood there by the sink, breathing in that smell and feeling something turning over inside me.

More February

Three children sliding on the ice
upon a summer's day –
it so fell out, they all fell in.
The rest they ran away.
Now, had these children been at home
or sliding on dry ground,
ten thousand pounds to one,
they had not all been drowned.
You parents that have children dear,
pray keep them safe at home.

What a terrible song! I'm sorry I just can't help it, singing it
I mean, it's stuck right in my head and I can't get it out. Who
sings that sort of thing to a child I can't imagine. I only
thought that maybe if I sang it just now it would help. Isn't it
true that sometimes, saying a thing is helpful when we're trying
to get it to leave us alone? Honestly though, it must have been

written by a mother, that song I mean, who else imagines her children drowning under the ice in the middle of summer?

You know the woman who sleeps here? In the bed under the window? She's getting her teeth cleaned right now. Or fixed maybe. They took her out this morning. They said maybe there's a problem with her jaw and that's why she won't talk. Or maybe a problem with her teeth and that's why she keeps her mouth closed all the time except when she's asleep.

They're going to drive her somewhere to be looked at. They said that to her on the way out. We're going in a car. They were talking to her like some people talk to cats, when they know the cat is listening but know also that it can't understand words. They talk to me like that too. When they talk to me at all. Always saying everything twice.

It's true, that she never talks, or looks at anyone. She won't talk to me about anything, she just sits in her chair all day and grows whiskers.

Listen, please, I need you to ask them something. Please. They don't listen to me. They say I'm not ready to be listened to yet. In terms of requests they must mean. That I haven't earned that or them. Something like that. So I need you to ask them to stop letting her daughter into our room. I need them to stop.

When they let her daughter in, her daughter, who's older than me and fat and wears overalls and squelching yellow rubber boots, goes over to her and kisses her on the cheek. Then she braids her hair, her mother's hair I mean, into these two limp braids that she leaves coiled in her lap, her mother's lap. Do you see? And she never looks up, the mother I mean, the woman in the bed under the window. She never looks up at her daughter, and her daughter never looks over at me. When they're there, by the window together, well I can't really tell you. Well I can't. Not really.

I can only say that I curl up into a ball on the edge of my bed or that I sometimes press my head into my pillow and scream or make noises but only like a bird would. Like a crow. Caw caw caw. And I shout. I find myself shouting, Love Cannot Save You. But it only comes out in crow. Caw caw. Caw caw caw. Like retching. It sounds funny now, but I can't help it when she's here in the room. The woman's fat daughter. It can't go on. You have to tell them that. I shall lose my voice or I shall turn into a bird or I shall peck out all my hair looking for feathers. Do you see it? My hair? It's already in patches. No. It's all right. Right now it's all right. I'm calm. See? I have something else to talk to you about.

Do you have a moment? Caw. No, I'm kidding. Why are patients not allowed to tell jokes? Of all the things they take from us that might be the worst. To be always assumed to be serious. It's terrible. Listen though, one minute, please. I want to tell you.

There was a boy who lived in the house across from mine when I was little. I want you to be able to see it – my house. It was a big house. I had a pink bed with pink sheets and a bedroom with pink walls. I would watch this boy from my window. He had thick dark hair and dark eyes and he lived alone with his mother in a brick house that had a path leading from the driveway to the front door. On both sides of the path there were rose bushes. Every evening he would come out into the front garden with his mother and tend to them. They each had a small basket and a pair of pruning shears, his smaller than hers, and they would walk slowly through the flowers snipping or trimming or sometimes only just touching until all the roses had been seen to. Then they would walk in again together through the front door. Do you know when I picture them now they're wearing hats, old-fashioned things. Like gauzy boats sailing on top of their heads, old-fashioned hats for beekeepers they must be. But it wasn't really like that. Not really, it's only that I see them that way, now.

It's funny, I spent so much time watching them with the roses, but I couldn't imagine what they were like inside their house. If the mother maybe whispered terrible things to the little boy once the door was closed. Or if she made him his favourite dinner every night. I couldn't imagine it! Anyway, later the boy *chopped up all the roses into tiny pieces with his smaller shears. I know because I watched him do it through my pink curtains, crouching on my bed.*

You know I'm sorry really, to talk to you like this, perhaps you'd like it quiet. As quiet maybe as if we had all been painted up into a picture and our lips couldn't move anymore ever, as if our mouths had dried closed. Perhaps you'd like that. There.

Oh but I can't just sit here and be quiet! It feels so unfriendly. Is it silly that I feel like a hostess when you come in? It also feels like I've got something trying to crawl out of the front of my skull. Something pushing at me from the inside. Some awful wildness. But perhaps that's more to be expected in a place like this. A home like this I should say, considering we have a window.

Let's pretend everything was otherwise. Let's pretend we have nothing behind us. See? A game.

I will say, when you come in, into my room in this house, I will say, But where are my manners? Like this, with my hand here. And then I will say, Here, let me take your coat. Let me bring you a drink. Let me tuck that piece of hair back behind your ear because we're friends, best friends even, and it's nothing, really nothing, if I touch the side of your face with my fingers.

If I laugh a bit and dust a piece of something or other off the shoulder of your dress. If I lean into you just a bit if I'm jittery or tired. See? Because we're just like that, aren't we? We don't have to be too careful around each other.

They tell me I must talk to them in order to make progress, so perhaps it's right, perhaps I'm doing the right thing by talking to you. Do you think so? Only they tell me too that there's a right kind of talking. That there are things I need to talk to them about. I laughed and tried to make them laugh, just to try and lighten the mood, do you see? It's so serious in there, in their office with the heavy chairs and me with these silly old cuffs around my ankles. Clunking and hissing. Swishing like the bottom of a ballgown maybe, against an oiled parquet floor with wax as thick as ice. Lord we know what we are. But not, oh how does it go? Anyway, in there I seem ridiculous. I feel it. They don't laugh though. They only give me more pills, more appointments, and scribble down my jokes into their grim black notebooks.

Maybe, I screamed at them, the last time, in their offices, before I left, when they were telling me again and again, with their pens poised just above their notebooks, what it is that I need to talk to them about. Maybe I am already talking about those things, I screamed, Maybe I'm talking about those things all the time.

10

We had to go to the shops then, for the baby gift. The nice ones on Rue de Rive. Afterwards I could check on M's suits at the dry cleaners. I wanted to go to the park. I wanted to look for Nell. I filled containers with sliced cucumbers, tomatoes, a bottle of water, diapers and outfit changes, thousands of small packages each with their own lid snapped tight against all possible disasters.

I was in a hurry, for once, to leave, so I pulled the long coat from M over my stained saggy shirt, so thin and colourless as to be almost nothing, and pulled the beautiful camel-coloured lapels up close to my neck. Under the coat I could have been anyone. Anything. An elegant lady with a silk lace bra hugging her ribs, a jackal with a woman's face, anything at all.

E had dressed herself, as usual. I felt monstrous but out we went. I was tired today in a way that made my face feel strange, peeled open almost. The coat was too heavy and wrapped up inside it, I immediately began to sweat. E ran toward the tram stop and I called for her to stopstopstop, but she skipped ahead without turning back.

The boutiques were sprinkled up and down the beautiful old street. E and B and I began ducking in and out of them looking for a gift, me practising the way one should smile on entering, on leaving. The little curl up at the corners of the mouth. Not too much, just a bit. Bonjour I would say when someone said bonjour to me.

In one of the shops, E and I and B in his stroller found a small table on which baby things were displayed. Fat-bottomed baby pants, white bonnets, everything plush, everything tiny. Wooden animals painted in soft colours, their noses sanded down, their teeth blunted, made delightful. Rattles filled with wooden beads tuned to sound like spring rain. Everything was expensive. I picked out a set of small white cloth squares tied with linen and a wooden elephant with an upcurled trunk. Then I drifted over to another part of the store to solve the problem of wrapping everything up.

I could feel E tugging at my coat, pulling me over to look at something or other that had caught her eye. But if I could only find the correct paper, the right ribbon, I would resolve this for myself. I was doing something that needed to be done. I gazed at the ribbons for a long time, the mounds of smooth coils, my eyes floating over the blues and greens, the pinks were numerous but none of them right. One was too soft, another too brash, needy: all elbows. The wrapping papers, displayed half unrolled, fluttered like eyelids or butterfly wings.

E, it seemed, had run off. I called her name, but without lifting my eyes from the tissue paper, the ribbons. Images of large hands finding hers and leading her away, out of the store, a pink tuft disappearing around the corner and out the door flew across my mind. But still, that was nonsense, and I was busy doing this. B was sleeping in his bassinet and I should continue doing this necessary and important thing. I should for once not let myself succumb to everyday hysteria, to the thoughts of disaster that pressed themselves up against me, up against my face.

Next to the ribbons and papers the shop ladies were arranging silk wraps in a display. The wraps kept escaping their hangers and sliding to the ground, as if they were alive, as if they could run away from the ladies who were trying to hang them. E, I called out, but softly, so as not to disturb the quiet shop. E didn't answer. The ladies continued to try to arrange the wraps. One, a beautiful blue-grey wrap, embroidered with cranes, the birds all wide wings, necks turned upwards, a flash of red at the throat, fell at my feet.

I felt I really had lost E. I couldn't see her, but the cool silk pooled at my feet like a pond hidden in the forest, touching my bare ankle, inviting me in. E, I called softly. E, where are you? But my eyes were on the silk, not quite blue, not quite grey, a colour completely lost within itself. The cranes stared up at me with their crooked necks. I bent down to pick it up. B squirmed in his stroller, buried in a nest of pink ribbons I hadn't realized I'd taken, his hands coiled in them, fighting. The ribbons dangerous as snakes, my baby, buried in a nest of flicking tongues.

But I continued to run my hands through the silk. The shop ladies, seeing me, laid aside the other wraps, letting them slide to the floor like so many sighs. They turned to me, their eyes newly bright. They smiled at me with their painted jewel lips. I flipped over the price tag, the number made me sick, but I smiled back at the ladies. I could smile too, like them, in my beautiful coat. I took a step towards the register, leaving B, leaving all the ribbons, leaving the baby gift in the bottom of the stroller. I took a step as if I were a crane stretching out my long wings, my feet about to leave the cold surface of the pond.

There was a commotion behind me. A voice boomed, loud and insistent. I turned to find a large carelessly dressed woman holding E by the hand. I'm looking for her mother, the woman was saying, or something like that. She was out on the street, a child out alone on the street! She was speaking French, but she could have been saying that. I let the silk wrap slide from my fingers onto the cool black expanse of a table and went to gather my daughter up in my arms. The woman glared at me, the shop ladies had lost their pretty smiles. I quickly bought the baby's present and one of the pink ribbons and left.

We played in the hot park all afternoon and E managed to get a sunburn despite my attentions. Nell didn't come. Perhaps she would never come back. Perhaps that man had killed her.

That night in bed with B it felt as if aphids were crawling under my skin. Beading there. My heart buzzed under the sheets like a hive, choked by veins, by blood fighting its way out of my chest. I couldn't sleep. B was awake every hour, hungry, or too hot, or dreaming bad baby dreams.

It seemed that our two bodies were never not touching, would never not be. He was so hot in the hot apartment. I wanted to oil the floor in the guest room but he would not be put down, his small body burrowed next to mine. One moment he was like a soft-eared lion cub and the next he was like those blind maggots that seek out gangrenous wounds. I could never be sure in any minute which he would be, which I would. When he finally slept I slipped him into the crib and collapsed by the door of the guest room without opening it, without even raising my hand to the handle, and imagined that if I did open it, there would be a quiet ocean waiting inside with water salty enough to strip away everything that was unwanted from my skin.

I had begun to realize, or, really, to feel that there was something with me in the apartment. There was something that had slipped in somehow, through the locked door or through the window. The apartment was shifting I felt, turning, rolling over, opening up its arms, welcoming this thing that was not a person. Not M. This thing that was something slippery, something that smelled like dirt.

Maybe I was all wrong though, maybe it was nothing. Maybe it was just my phone, lost somewhere, buzzing, keeping me half awake. Maybe M was calling me. Maybe he was calling me often.

It was so dark and so quiet. I could hear B breathing in his crib.

There was a change in the air inside the apartment. I felt it and then I felt that there was almost surely something in the apartment with me, slipping, keeping just in the corners of my eyes, one moment too light, like the shadow of a child, the next too heavy, a toad, a slimy thing burping out an underground musk. I became very still where I was on the floor pushed up against the door of the guest room. Would I get up? Would I run, now, right now when it was important? When it was important to my children? Would I save them? With this wrong thing sneaking in the dark? Surely I would.

I waited and waited. What I'm trying to tell you is that I waited such a long time to find out if I would, if I would save them I mean. I passed through the whole night like this, crouching, waiting, watching myself to see what I would do.

There must have been a part of the night that passed without me realizing, because the next thing I knew, it was morning and I was waking up. I was pressed against the door of the guest room with my neck and shoulders horribly cramped, almost unmovable. I was waking up and it was morning and, well, I could feel that the thing was over. Whatever it had been. It was over, poof and gone like dust and I could stand and stretch and run my fingers through my hair. Hah! I could say. Hah! It was like standing on the top of a mountain, me saying it, the words all bold and free on my lips.

B woke up and was hungry. E woke up and was hungry. There were red marks on their faces and arms, a heat rash or kisses. We were out of yogurt. I got them ready and we all stumbled to the little store, half in our pyjamas and half out.

We filled our basket with warm croissants and almonds and milk from Gruyères, just because we could fill our basket with things like that. E found a package of lace-like cheese cut fine and curled in on itself, arranged behind its plastic window to look like flowers. We bought that too even though it was six francs because we were lucky and happy and when the checkout girl asked me if I'd found everything I was looking for, I nodded and said, Oui, merci, because we had. And also because miraculously, I'd understood what she'd said to me. Then she touched the side of her face and said something I didn't understand, so I only smiled and said have a good day with my best words and my careful accent, Bonne journée, I said, like that, and took the plastic handles of the bag and left.

We ate breakfast by the pump. We ate yogurt with our fingers and uncurled the little cheese flowers with our teeth. We tore up the croissants and watched all the hot little pieces fall to the ground. We could behave like this, like wolves, because we had the whole place to ourselves.

I let B nap in the grass beside the pump. I let E cover up my feet with handfuls of sand a hundred times and when she looked up and said, Ready, I held my face and moaned. Oh my god, I said a hundred times. Oh my god where have my feet gone. Then E would find them for me, scraping away the sand from my toes and I hugged her, a hundred times. Oh I was so worried, I said a hundred times. I thought I'd lost them. Other women began showing up at the park mid-morning with their children, their strollers, their tiny buckets and shovels. I thought we should go back and get dressed but I also thought, a quick flash that wasn't even really a thought, we should not go back, we should not go back to the apartment. We should not go back to that place. Besides, B was still asleep and E was saying please stay, please please stay. Sometimes being a good mother was just staying right where you were. So I leaned back into the pump and we played the game with my feet again and again and again. Some mornings could be like this if you let them.

Later, Nell came to the park. She walked right past me, close enough that I could smell her perfume. She opened her blanket and laid it out on the grass beside B, unwrapped the baby and put him down on it. I watched her carefully because I wanted to make sure that she was all right. I checked her arms for bruises, things like that, but there was nothing. She was humming some song to her baby, the older boy was already playing at the pump. Looking for him, her eyes caught on me and widened for a moment and she touched her cheek.

She was going to say something to me. She was going to say something to me and after all this time we were going to be friends, we were going to help each other easily. Can you? I'd say, reaching for something, and she would be able to reach it and hand it to me. The baby cried and Nell turned to him, whispering something in his ear. She turned back to me and touched her face, and the look in her eyes then was distant and a little afraid.

It was time to go. I stood up, not wanting anymore to linger, to be looked at. I collected E, crying now that we had to leave, tugging on my arm, really pulling me, and B who had been beginning to cry already, and we left the park. I regretted that we'd been there, put ourselves outside of the apartment to be seen and watched and spoken to.

Back inside the apartment I went into the bathroom and looked in the mirror. The side of my face was covered in a dark spreading bruise. Purple black and yellow, swollen even, with veins spidering out, blood running away, or to it, depending.

There were small bruises on my left arm below the elbow. Like the shadows of blackberries, I thought. Like there is a vine growing inside my arm and the fruit is finally ready to come out. But of course, of course, I knew these marks were fingerprints, long oval fingerprints. Of course also, I knew that my arm must look exactly like Nell's arm had, after that man, her man, had grabbed her in the park. I hadn't felt a thing all day, but now looking in the mirror, my fingers touching my cheek just as Nell had touched her own, just as, I now realized, the checkout girl at the store had touched hers, I could feel how my cheek was. I could feel the bruise now, pulsing under my fingertips as if it were a thing complete with its own heart.

E was calling me. Calling me and calling me and calling me. I ran out of the bathroom. She was standing in the hallway holding lemons. The baby giraffe was thirsty, wanted lemonade. Could I make it? Her voice was fuzzy, far away, I could hardly hear it. I pressed my hands to my chest and calmed myself down. Overreactions were common enough, the point was to remain quiet about them.

I walked to the kitchen and made lemonade, cups and cups and cups of it, mashing the lemons down onto the rental-company citrus squeezer until the little reservoir underneath was overflowing with juice and seeds and the counter was covered with lemon rinds, cracked open like sticky yellow egg shells. It was so hot. All the windows were closed tight but the flies still found a way in, buzzing around me the moment I tried to sit down or close my eyes. They walked all over everything. They touched us all over with their dancing feet. We could feel them all the time on our skin.

E and I played Amazon jungle with the baby giraffe. We pretended the raft would only take two of us, that there were red-bellied piranhas in the water, night on its way and all sorts of other terrible things. A decision would have to be made or none of us would make it out alive. The raft was simply not sufficient. E smiled her wicked smile, and hugged me tight.

More and More February

Can I tell you about my mother's Christmas parties? Would you stay so I can tell you? It's just so grey out today and I'm all alone and it feels like I'm tied up and drowning in this gown. Like a fish caught in a net. And I suppose that makes them, and you too really, trawlers doesn't it? Where are you pulling all of us fish I wonder?

Really though. Would you stay? Just a bit longer. What if I kicked over my water glass? Would you stay then? To clean it up? Oh, that was horrible of me to say. Really, I'm sorry. I feel that we're much more than that to each other. Much more than kicking feet and cleaning hands. I hope I can be more than that. Please stay. For just a moment. She's at treatment now, the woman in the bed under the window, so it's just the two of us.

Just the two of us girls. Someone might say that about us, if they peeked in. Oh, they might say, it's just the two of you girls.

Would you listen? Mother gave the most wonderful Christmas parties. All the neighbours came. It was as if the house became a paper lantern, I always thought of it like that, in December. One of those lanterns with a candle inside that gets released up into the sky. It was all that perfect and that delicate. Nothing could be touched inside the house in December, while Mother got it ready for the party. The mantel was set with white cotton and decorated with Santa and his reindeer. The table was covered over with the best white tablecloth from Paris and set, the week before the party, with the nutcracker plates and fresh pine boughs and red poinsettias and, in the middle, the red and gold punch bowl from Hermès. Mother always said it just like that. A bit breathlessly. Hermès. She would lift her right hand to touch just here, just under her throat, when she said it. I don't know if she knew that she did that. The punch bowl from Hermès. She would say it just like that. I want you to hear her saying it. Her voice, her breathlessness. It feels so important for you to understand.

My favourites though were the little houses that Mother set out along the windowsill. The Christmas village. One house with red shutters, one with green, one with blue and all with white painted snow and perfect lines of icicles just under the little roofs. There was a bakery too, with painted cakes in the window and an ice-skating pond where little ceramic children wearing tiny ceramic skates were glued to a track. At the flick of a switch the houses would light up with real electric lights and the tiny children would loop and loop and loop around the same track for ever, as long as anyone wanted them to.

What I mean to say was, inside December, inside my house, inside the party, there was a switch. A switch that could be turned on, and it was magical and wonderful and real. As real as plugs and electricity and engineering. At the party, Daddy would be home all day and my mother would wear a new dress and they would even dance, just a moment but laughing. If the right song came on late in the afternoon. I remember his hand on her back, guiding her around the living room in circles, like the ice-skating children. I remember all the smiling. The punch. Parties can be like that, can't they? A place where anything is possible.

Mother didn't keep the punch bowl after Daddy left. It's possible that she broke it. It's possible that she picked it up and smashed it on the driveway at night. On the night after the last party. After all the guests had left, after he was leaving. I just have to go, he said. I have to go I have to go I have to go. I can't do this anymore. It's possible that she followed him, in her dress, in her dress that she had danced in, in the dress that was possibly still warm in the place on her back where he had put his hand when they were dancing, down the steps from the front door carrying the huge red bowl sloshing with the last of the punch, sloshing up onto her dress in dark red waves. A wine-dark sea so small you could miss it, if you weren't watching it with your nose pressed up to the window. So small and furious. It would have been quite possible to miss the way the punch sloshed up onto the dress and stained the dress's red a redder red and made it so that you could see the soft indent of her belly button through the silk. It's possible that she raised the punch bowl up over her head and threw it at his car as he pulled out of the driveway and it's possible that it all smashed on the drive. The sea, the punch bowl from Hermès. And if it really had been a sea, inside the bowl, all the men on all the boats would have been instantly killed. Can you see it? The wreckage of all those little boats?

Anyway, that was the end of the parties. But we set up the village, in our new apartment. The Christmas village. Actually, if you want to know, Mother put a board over the black metal bed frame in her room. A big pine board that she found in the parking lot behind our new apartment complex, that was better, she said, than our old house, because it had a pool and a community game room, and she set the village up on that, on the board I mean. We sprayed the board white one afternoon, soon after we moved in, and she brought out the Christmas box as a surprise and set up the little houses even though it was July, and said, See? We can live like we want to now! We can do anything! Anything is possible now. Now that we are here. We slept in sleeping bags together underneath the bed with the Christmas village on top of it for months and months and months. We even left *the lights on in the houses all night long so they would speckle the dark walls in the new apartment. We loved to fall asleep to the whirring of the ceramic children skating on the plastic ice. We were waiting you see, for everything to happen.*

You mustn't imagine, my mother said to me once from our hiding place under the Christmas bed, you mustn't imagine that I'm not any fun. You mustn't imagine that we can't now have wonderfully good times right here. I can remember her voice, the way she said it to me. The way it sounded exactly as if she was asking me to give her something back.

There's something about December for me I suppose, it seems like a place, an island maybe, and January means leaving and February means having left. And here we are. I only wanted to tell you I suppose, because of that.

It seems silly, to talk about Christmas parties, about my mother. Maybe you think so too. Maybe you think it's quite silly. I tried to tell the doctor about the Christmas parties, about my mother, the village, the dress, but he wouldn't listen. I said, and I was trying to be funny, But aren't you supposed to talk about your mother in places like this? But he didn't laugh. He didn't laugh so much that it was the opposite of laughing. What is that? I can't think of the word for it, for the opposite of laughing, but it's something isn't it, that leaves one quite alone. He said, clicking his black and gold Montblanc pen, that there were other things to talk about and I said, I was only making a joke! And he said this is not the place for jokes and I said, Honestly! And he said, Honestly.

11

I had the gift for the baby on the table by the door. The gift was just right. M would be home after dinner tonight, I could feel it. I was so certain that he would.

I boiled water for pasta and didn't walk away from it for a single second while it came up, while it was a dangerous thing. I watched it like a good mother, well I was! I gave E a bowl of warm strozzapreti with tiny slices of tomato and carrot sprinkled on top. Here we are, I said when I set the bowls down on the table and I could hear the way my mother would have said it. The way she had said it a thousand thousand times.

After E went to sleep, after B had been fed and put into his crib, I cleaned the counters and wiped the dirty places underneath the refrigerator. I wiped down all the doorknobs with vinegar and water. I cleaned the sink in the guest room and turned the plant a quarter turn, gave it a little water. I couldn't understand how it could breathe in there, shut up in that dark little room that should be so different, that would be, after I had made it right.

I wanted to be awake and dressed and ready to talk to M about his day when he came home. To ask a question maybe, how was this or that going. Had this important thing happened? Or that?

When I had first stopped working, when E was a baby and I found myself suddenly at home all alone with her, saying goodbye to M at the door, I found myself wondering, during the day, if I should pick up his socks, do his laundry. If I should now, if I was now obligated to. Only when the paychecks had stopped coming in the mail, flimsy funny things and not ever for very much money but printed anyhow with my name on them and no one else's, did the weight of them become, to me, clear. Not until they were gone and I no longer had to get dressed or even go outside really. Until I just had to stay where I was every second and make sure that the baby wasn't killed in one of the many many ways I had been told it was possible for such a thing to happen.

Once, when E was four months old, she reached for something, a toy, her stuffed octopus maybe, and got it in her hands. It was the first time she'd ever done that, reached for something and grabbed it. My heart leapt outside of myself. It was the most amazing thing, is the most amazing thing, I have ever ever seen. My daughter doing this, and I grabbed my phone and called him, called M at the office with tears in my eyes and tried to explain the thing that had just happened but as soon as the words left my mouth I saw that I never should have done it. Should never have called him like that.

Wow! he said, That's great, but his voice was soft and I kept trying to explain what had happened even though I'd already told him, even though he already knew, even though I could hear the sound of keyboards tapping in the background. Even though I was seeing with creeping horror how silly I was showing myself to be, how tiny and bathrobed and silly and alone, and he said more quietly, That's great, we'll talk about it tonight. I'm so sorry, I have to go, he said, I love you. He said all these things that were of course exactly right and it was only me who was silly for calling. Yes, I said, of course, I said, and I was so angry for showing myself in that way. For allowing myself to be seen as I was.

I put on an impractical skirt, an old shirt that almost fit, and sat in the kitchen and sipped a brandy until it was so late that being dressed and waiting felt ridiculous. Then I was relieved that he hadn't come back after all and I changed back into my apartment clothes and crumpled up in some corner or other. After a while of steady breathing I fell into something that was not quite sleeping but resting. Dreaming in a half dreaming sort of way. There was, in my dream or out of it, the something again, the something in the apartment with me, the something that wasn't M, that was like a cross between a child and a toad. A thing that maybe could laugh a high little laugh and hide in all the corners of the apartment.

In my dream I was running through the rooms of the apartment. E and B were asleep. I was running to the door, the front door that would let me out, but I was never going to make it because I wasn't fast enough, because I was carrying the plant in my arms, because its thick green tentacles were slowing me down, slithering along the floor, catching on things. I tripped on something, a toy or a bowl of lemons and fell to the ground. The plant turned to sand in my fingers. The clay of the pot. The thick green stalks. It all melted into the same mess, running through my fingers until there was nothing left.

I woke breathing hard, light slipping in through the shutters. It was yet again and always again and more and more another morning and I'd hardly slept at all. I was losing track of things. Also I was angry at my dreaming self and disappointed.

My dream-self was, I supposed, a terrible mother, no kind of mother at all. My dream-self had been running for the door with the plant in her arms. My dream-self had been leaving her children. Who could have said what would happen if she had gotten her fingers on the handle of the door? Or really I knew. I could have said. I would have been gone.

The morning raked across my exhausted face, there were fresh bruises on my knees and shins. Maybe I had been really running, really stumbling, last night when I had or hadn't been sleeping.

I ran to the bathroom to take a shower. I felt that if I was not, at that moment, able to rip off all my clothes and jump into the shower and wash away all my sweat and terrible mother dreams I would begin to scream and if I began to scream I felt perhaps that I would never stop.

When I was a child I remember loving to play house which meant mostly playing that I had many babies, at least three or four, to look after. I would wipe their mouths with soft little squares of fabric that my mother cut for me from old clothes and I would change their diapers by tying and untying other squares of fabric around their moulded plastic bottoms. The babies were always almost asleep in my games, always equally ready to be put down and left or picked up and cuddled. They were always girls, dressed in pink with names like Diamond, Rainbow, Butterfly, depending on my mood.

I was so patient with them, telling them the names of things, pointing out to them what was important, what mattered, what should matter. I thought of the way we would be when the babies were older, we would all be young and beautiful together, like sisters, only with me the most beautiful, the most loved. We would all have long hair that I would comb and braid. Our hair would be thick and golden. We would all be the same height, we would all have the hard, concave waists of dolls.

It was a bit like I, as a child, had thought it would be, when E was born. I taught her all the names of things. Everything about her was a gift from me, from my body. I had made her out of nothing. When she got older though I saw already that I was quickly being broken down for parts. I saw also that I was not the one who would choose my useful pieces. My hands, which were only months ago the hands that brought the world to her, which shaped it and allowed it to exist for her, were suddenly only good for sorting laundry, for scrubbing the hardened crust on a forgotten dish. Well and why should anything be any different. Mothers were mothers, whether we were lying down, torn apart, in a heap of scraps, or tall and standing and all in one piece. Either way, the hands that scrubbed the dishes were loving ones.

When I was pregnant with B, I slept all the time, and when I dreamed, I dreamed of girls standing on the edge of a lake, peeling off pieces of themselves like sweaters and sealing them up into neat little packages and setting them on the surface of the water and with a breath, whoosh, sending them away. Sometimes I could see even when I was awake, the surface of a lake covered with tidy floating boxes. Pregnancy does strange things, I was told by my doctor, to the body. He cautioned me that I must smile and behave cheerfully around E, that I must avoid being nervous, that I must avoid eating tuna, that I must avoid undercooked meat.

I braided my hair while I waited for E and B to wake up, even though I was too old to wear it in braids, as if I were a girl. Even though it made me look older still than I was, bringing out the shallow wrinkles at the corners of my eyes, the deepening lines around my mouth. The bruise on my cheek was yellowing, making my face look like a map for tiny boats to sail on, my eyes becoming the inlets or maybe the whirlpools, safe havens, or maybe something else.

Perhaps the braids made me look chic. Perhaps I would wear my hair like this to give the baby gift this weekend. I would of course have to wear foundation to cover the bruise. It was Friday morning, we would have to go tomorrow. M and I and B and E to the apartment on the other side of the lake. It was Friday which meant that M would surely have to come home tonight.

I took a bottle of pills out from the medicine cabinet and swallowed one or two, I had certainly, only just a moment ago felt a headache, or the shadow of a headache gathering, I almost certainly had. It was good to take care of these things as soon as possible. I cleaned my teeth then opened the bathroom door to screaming and ran off forgetting the braids and the headache to make breakfast, then lunch, and snacks and dinner. Tonight would be different, M would be home. Today I could cook dinner and clean the apartment and love the children and be just the thing that would make everything right. Like a wonderful vase that sets a room off in just the right way. I could be the vase and also the person who cleaned it. If I worked hard and loved the children and M came home to us, everything would be right.

I was tired that afternoon beside the pump and almost asleep on the blanket with B when Nell came to the park.

She looked tired too and different than she normally did. Her hair wasn't brushed to its usual gloss. The strap of her dress was slipping off one shoulder in a way she didn't seem to want it to. She was patient still with the children. She passed them the toys from her pockets when they asked but she sat listlessly on the side of the blanket and picked at the frayed edges of it when they weren't looking.

I could answer questions now in French, simple ones, but I couldn't ask them. The formulations were too hard. I was too liable to get lost inside the sentences. She had new shoes on her tiny feet, yellow ones with a pattern pricked into the leather that I would have had to be quite close beside her to really see well. She had dark shadows under her eyes that rested there like moth wings. What I mean to say is that they were delicate, the shadows, all done up in various soft greys. I expected to see bruises, honestly I was looking for them, but there wasn't anything to see. Nothing besides those delicate shadows. I wanted things to make sense but I couldn't piece them out.

I left the pump before she did. I was busy, I had dinner to make, a table that was hungry for it. The other mothers sensed it too, and we all began gathering our things, our ears twitching like deer, moving as a herd, all of us feeling the ropes and strings and pulleys connecting us to our pots and pans and washing machines grow taut around our wrists. But Nell only played with the baby's hair, handed things to the boy, as I hurried off with the other mothers.

140

I made pasta for dinner, a sauce with fresh tomatoes and basil, M's favourite. The apartment smelled like a hot hill in Tuscany. I opened a bottle of red wine and let it breathe. E fed her animals sesame seeds one by one, dripping them carefully into their plastic mouths as if they were tiny drops of milk. They spilled on the floor and I saw this but didn't chastise her like a hateful stingy mother would but smiled at her and loved everyone.

I thought we could make cookies for Daddy! I said to E, who didn't look up, so I said it again to B and squished my nose up against his, wrinkling it in exactly the way I had done in a picture that I loved of myself from when I was eighteen. B gurgled at me and I turned back to the kitchen to get the dough ready. It was so hot in the apartment that the butter was melting already, slumping, oozing out across the counter in a bright slick.

I scooped the whole mess into a bowl and added flour and eggs and sugar and stirred it with a wooden spoon in exactly the way I had imagined I would. The dough smelled good and was soft in my hands. I pinched off a piece and ate it. I crushed the sugar crystals between my teeth and ate another piece, then another.

B began to cry, he had been crying and crying all afternoon and now he was crying again. I felt suddenly choked and instead of turning to pick him up, I took a big handful of dough, almost all of it really, and mashed it into my mouth. For a second I couldn't breathe. I wondered if I would choke to death but it passed, the giant gob of dough, down my throat and I ran fast to get the baby. I sat with him whoosh down on the sofa and slipped my nipple into his hungry little mouth. Good mother. Bad mother. Good. Bad. A coin flipped high in the air, spinning up and up and up.

I brought my fingers across my forehead to smooth away the wrinkles, to bring my face back in order. I used one hand to relax my jaw while I held B in the crook of my arm. I could hear myself breathing, a heehawing sound that I realized was strange even as I couldn't stop myself from doing it. I realized I was crying and also that I was still wearing my hair in the braids, that I had gone around all day looking like some terrible doll with an old woman's face, all lined and wrinkled. I realized this and then felt silly and pulled my nipple out of B's mouth, set him down on the carpet and went to see what was left of the cookie dough. Just enough. I put it in the fridge to firm up and went into the bathroom to undo my hair and put it up in some way that was less terrible, some way that made it clear that I knew what I was.

B was crying again but I found this time I could smile and walk to him without shaking and pick him up and hold him and sing a song to him without the words coming out of my mouth too loudly or too quickly. He smiled at me and I hugged him and I felt again saved from something ghastly and there we were rocking and singing and ready to be watched again, ready to be seen.

When I was little, maybe four, maybe five, I had a butter-scotch coloured mouse and I would cuddle it and play with it and carry it with me around our house in the pocket of my shirt. It would sit on my shoulders sometimes and make a nest in my hair and I could hear it hiding and chewing and squeaking a little. It had a cage with a blue ceramic bowl for its pellets and a water bottle that I decorated with stickers. I didn't play with it when I was alone though, I wasn't old enough. My mother watched me.

Until she didn't, until one day she wasn't there and I got out the mouse and played with it and it bit me so hard that I squeezed it and it went limp in my hands and I put it back inside its cage and left it there and waited for it to wake up. Of course it didn't, and we buried it under the plum tree in our front yard. The whole summer I watched the plums on that tree fatten, turning from green to dark purple to almost black. In the late summer, when we ate them, they were the most delicious plums we'd ever tasted. The best that had ever grown on that old tree. Perhaps my mother and I decided then that we were forgiven and who anyway is to say forgive-ness isn't a thing we all deserve? The plums were so good that we ate them for months, in pies, in jam, and fresh too, all on their own, sitting at the base of the tree with the juice running down our cheeks, our chins, our arms.

It was getting late. I tried to hold dinner so we could all eat together but the pasta was going hard on the top and grey at the bottom while we waited and the sauce was bubbling away to nothing on the back of the stove. In the end it did, bubble away to nothing, and the tomatoes burned and stuck to the bottom of the pot. I gave E a slimy plate of cold pasta and hoped that M wouldn't come home before everything could be cleaned up, the pot scrubbed, dinner cleared away.

At least we could still make the cookies. It was my mother's recipe, the cookie dough, which she had gotten from her mother, so there were always comparisons, glances, the taking of tiny bites, the saying of nice things. Only I was the only one here now making it. I pulled the dough out of the refrigerator and E jumped up, greedy for it, grabbing at me at the bowl all at once and this was of course really such a wonderful thing, that she was happy, jumping. I jumped too a little bit to show that I thought this was all wonderful. We rolled the dough out into little balls and I let her press them into any shape that she wanted to.

E was flattening them in ways that would never bake correctly, too thick on one side, too thin in the middle, but I didn't mention this. I only tried to fix them up a little once she put them down on the tray, saying all the time of course how nice they looked. How perfect. How much Daddy would love them. I was sweating a little bit, just at my hairline.

B began to cry in the other room. It was maybe ten o'clock and the cookies weren't finished and I was still alone in the apartment with the children. Children who should have been in bed. Children who would in the morning be so tired, who would not sleep well at all. Who would not sleep perhaps all night because of this, because of me letting them stay up so late.

My heart began to get out from under me. E was pressing on me, standing on my foot, her elbow digging into all the places I was still fat from having B, all the places that would never be the same.

I can't breathe! Suddenly I was shouting this, I can't breathe! Well, I really couldn't. I tried to make it a game, grabbing at my neck and making my eyes big but E had snapped back into herself and was watching me like she sometimes does, when she turns her eyes into ponds, liquid murky things, filled with frogs. Sometimes everything was like this and I couldn't be calm.

I left the cookies on the counter and took E to bed. Telling her all the time what a good girl she was, how much I loved her. Wishing I could calm my face down a bit, relax my jaw. I could feel my teeth almost turning to powder in my mouth I was biting down that hard. E held my hand delicately as I led her into her room and tucked her into bed. She was so far away from me, her eyes like tiny pinpricks of light. Christmas lights on a fishing boat when I was already deep underwater. I kissed her forehead and told her I loved her but I had to wipe the spot where my cheek had touched hers because I was sweating so much that it left a mark.

B was screaming now but I couldn't make myself go to him even though we were all supposed to be so quiet. I jumped in the shower with my clothes still on. Sometimes that sort of thing helped, like jumping as high as you could five times when no one was looking or pinching the inside of your legs or screaming into a pillow. The water was good. It was cold and it brought me back to myself. I could be calm.

I peeled my clothes off and left them in the bottom of the shower, wrapped a towel around my puckered-up supermarket chicken skin and went to pull on another pair of sweatpants, an old T-shirt. B was quiet now and this made me, of course, feel much worse and I ran to him and picked him up and told him I loved him I loved him I loved him even though he was almost now asleep and I was only bothering him. I slipped my nipple into his mouth and he obliged me by sucking a bit before falling back asleep and leaving me.

I wiped down the kitchen counters, threw away the unbaked cookies, cleaned the tray. I checked the floor and cabinets for bits of glass. At some point the voice would start talking to me behind the door and I didn't want to hear it. If I kept working perhaps I would be too busy to hear it. I sharpened the knives again against the stone, scritch scritch scritch, filing the metal to such a fine point. Eating up the minutes that way along with the edge of the blade.

I finished the knives, polished the cabinet handles, wiped down the awful red rental-company refrigerator, climbed up onto the table to wipe the greasy stick off the tops of the lights. My grandmother said a man once ran his fingers over the tops of the doors in her house before he tried to kiss her, wanting first to check, he told her, how she kept her house. Of course this was terrible but I wanted the tops of the lights clean regardless. I got tired anyway though and went over to the sofa, curled myself up behind a mountain of pillows and closed my eyes.

A moment later or maybe hours, M was there in the room with me, home, he looked tired and smelled a little bit of sweat. He reached into my stack of pillows and brought his face down and kissed me behind the ear. I love you, he said. I definitely heard him say it.

We had been so young together once, I hadn't forgotten a second of it. The being young. The way he had looked at me when we were in that golden country and had good hair and teeth and were supple just by nature and not by trying. When every day was a market and all the shelves were stocked. We could have anything we wanted! It was all true and had happened, though it was hard to believe any of it now with our life always piled up all around us in heaps and mounds, slumping and shifting, old laundry and recycling. But it was all fine now that he was home, the walls pushed back a little around me, around us both maybe and I slept.

12

We all dressed carefully the next morning. M was a little nervous, he put on the clothes he wore to the office. A shirt from Milan. He looked like himself now, in the collared shirt, which was strange because I could remember the first time he put on a suit and it looked too big and loose on him and I thought he could have walked by me on the street looking like that and I wouldn't have recognized him. If he saw the bruise, he didn't mention it. I was grateful for his consideration, but also it made me feel a little slippery inside, like maybe what was real didn't stay true and fixed from one day, from one minute, to the next. Or maybe it was that what was true and real for me wasn't true and real for both of us together. Or of course maybe it was just that I had done my make up well. How many things could be equally true all at once?

E wore a white dress with little eyelets strewn across the fabric like flower petals. They were meant to look careless, you paid extra for that kind of thing, for their perfect off-handedness. I brushed her hair and oiled it a little and braided it carefully. She always cried when I braided her hair, pulling this way and that, undoing the work that had been done, forcing us to start again, but I thought, I really thought that she would one day like to remember my fingers in her hair. I thought that she would remember this love, my love, here, even though she cried now and said it hurt. Isn't love sometimes like this? We're always setting ourselves up to remember it.

M dressed B, pulling his little kicking legs through a pair of pants, sliding them up over the fat diaper. The boys I would probably one day call them, and I would laugh and be a woman in her forties and I would roll my eyes a bit and cross my arms in front of myself and tap my foot. We would be a family with pet names for each other, we would be that happy.

I couldn't find anything to wear. I tried on shirt after shirt but none of them fit. The sleeves were too long, it was almost as if they might drag on the floor. The buttons were too tight. It was suddenly as if I were a grape being squashed down beside the rental-company bed by a monstrous thumb. I was bulging out, grinding down into the cheap carpet. I threw on a dress and ran out of the room, tripping, fast so the mirror couldn't catch me. I rubbed more foundation over the bruise on my face, dusted it with more powder. I was the last one to the door, the last one to leave the apartment but I was ready now. We all walked out into the hallway and M locked the door behind us. Immediately I wanted to be back inside. To spend the whole day curled up but M was there waiting and B would start to cry soon, would be hungry. So we left the building and walked to the tram stop. I was sorry it was too hot to wear my long coat.

M bought the tram tickets and slipped them into his pocket. When the tram came we all climbed on and rode it down the hill, past the train station and across the bridge over the lake. It was a beautiful day, we could have been in Paris in three hours. We got off the tram and walked past a flower shop where a young woman in a chequered apron was wrangling huge sunflowers with stalks as thick as her own wrists into an enormous bouquet. A bouquet that when lifted, made her, the tiny girl, look lost inside it. She was roping them together like cattle. M bought E a pink flower and she loved it, kissed it, crushed it and left it in the street all in the space of two minutes. Love was like that too of course. Blossoming and beautiful and bursting and delicate and gone. Why pretend otherwise?

We walked to M's boss's apartment building. It was one of the old-looking ones along the lake. It had a wrought-iron elevator in the lobby like a bird cage you closed yourself into. We rode it all the way to the top and stepped out in front of a tall white door with so much inlay and moulding that it looked like a maze, only it was perfectly made and so, of course, there was no way out. As we wrestled with the stroller, fighting with E who wanted to run ahead, M's boss's wife opened the door.

She was wearing a white dress that fell down her body like a waterfall, like a miracle, touching her just here and here. There was a panel cut out of one side, where a pocket would have been but which instead made a paneless window to a tan hip, the bone running just so. The perfect accessory, more unattainable than the latest this or that. A place for her, or for someone else to rest a hand. Oh this old thing, she could have said when she walked and showed it, how perfect it was, the dress, the hip. It was impossible to believe that she'd just had a baby, wearing white, wearing that dress.

M leaned in to kiss her cheeks, three times. It wasn't really kissing, more touching. They smiled at each other like people who have eaten dinner together. I could see this. As he leaned in to kiss her he touched her shoulder like a man who knew whether she liked a cocktail first, or wine. But of course they had all eaten together, many times after work. I knew this, that M's boss's wife often came along at night when they went to restaurants, meeting them after she left her office.

M's boss came out behind her, the baby on his shoulder, holding a hand out for M to shake. We were welcomed inside, walked through double doors, asked to sit. M took B out of the stroller and M and M's boss looked at each other and laughed. Tailored shirts, wool pants, leather shoes, men with things to do. Men who could at that moment have called any number of people, who had at that moment many things to do, and there they were holding babies. That was a cue for the women, meaning me and M's boss's wife, to smile at each other, to pass on some sort of congratulations to each other, here we were, two lucky women, something like that. We did smile, we took our cue just fine.

Just inside the door, E asked where the tea was, stamping her little patent-leathered foot, and so we were all given another opportunity, the adults I mean, to look at each other knowingly and laugh. There was often, almost always, only one way for these sorts of afternoons to proceed. The smiling, the laughing, the knowing looks, the hand held out just so, come in please!

We were taken through to the living room where M and M's boss sat down on the perfect French-blue sofa with the babies. They leaned back into the cushions and M's boss's wife and I, arranged in high-backed chairs around the occasional table, got down to the business of searching for something to talk about.

The gift we left on the side table in the entryway. It did look good there. The sunlight lay draped about the room like a member of the family, resplendent in a familiar way, at home and cuddled up in all the best places. The curtains hung down from the tall ceilings, light and airy, like the breath of beautiful women.

Of course I couldn't say any of this to M's boss's wife, the script was laid out for us and did not permit whimsical deviations. She would say something nice about E and I would thank her. I would laugh once or twice and compliment the rug. I would try to keep from tugging on my dress.

I would ask her where she got something or other and say I was looking for something like it. Something else would be hard to find, some bottle of cleaning spray, or decent coffee or bread, and we would note that and tut. I would take her advice and thank her. Of course I would ooh over the baby. I would say something about them growing up so fast and about how much I loved them, babies, all kinds.

She had an accent when she spoke but not a French one. She offered tea and so I had to ask how I could help. Then this, she had to refuse, No, no, no, she had to say. Please, stay just where you are.

We made out fairly well this way, keeping ourselves on well-oiled tracks. M and M's boss were talking, patting the backs of the babies while they slept. Soon one of us, M's boss's wife or me, would have to look at the husbands and say something. I would need to prepare a compliment, something about how my M liked his boss, or the work. I would have to say my M, affectionately, like that.

She left and came back with a teapot, poured tea into cups that were already set out. M and M's boss waved away the cups when they were offered and so we returned to the table and had to drink them even though it was too hot outside for tea. E had run off somewhere. I should go look for her I said, and M's boss's wife said, Stay, let her play and smiled as if we two knew all about the secret ways of children.

The table was set with a tray of macaroons in pastel colours. She offered me one and I took it and bit into it. I tried to pass the plate to her but she waved them away and said no she couldn't and the whole thing felt like a trick. I looked for E, I wanted to give the rest to her but I couldn't find her. I couldn't get up then though so I swallowed the second half and went back to the tea.

M's boss's wife had her phone on the table next to her and it kept buzzing. She flicked away a few calls with her manicured fingers, always turning back to me and smiling and apologizing, rolling her eyes a little. They're supposed to leave me alone! she said. She said something like that.

My eyes moved back and forth between her and her new baby. How could both be real? Her baby was so much younger than mine and yet she had those painted fingers, those people calling her on her phone, had that hip in that dress. Perhaps it all came down to the half-bottle of champagne mothers were given here in the clinics, after they give birth, the Descamps linens that lined the airy privately insured beds, perhaps these things that seemed so fine and frivolous were actually like graceful toeholds on the side of a cliff. Perhaps your baby was the ocean you would otherwise fall into, perhaps your baby's mouth was like the mouth of those birds where all the teeth point backwards, preventing escape, like those birds whose backwards pointing teeth continue all the way down their throats.

There was some art hung on the wall, hammered metal of some kind. The light reflected off it and lit her perfectly from behind, so she looked softened, like she had a glow about her. I thought about a piece of advice that I'd heard somewhere or other, that for a woman to look her best, she should pin a diamond into the lapel of her jacket. This was so that light, when it caught the diamond, would shine on her face softly, without other people realizing the trick. M's boss's wife was like that now, lit from behind, the light almost holding her up like Venus on her seashell. Well, she was beautiful like that. I wondered if she always sat in that chair, in that spot, in that light.

Text bubbles popped up on the screen of her phone and she glanced down a few times, pulled up her calendar, moved her thumb down the screen. They want me to fly to a meeting in Dubai, can you imagine? The answer was of course, No, I couldn't. But I said it anyway, No, I can't! Like that, and arranged my face to show I was surprised and impressed. To show I really couldn't imagine it. Sometimes of course the faces that we make are true.

She typed away into her phone and called over to M's boss eventually, saying something like, but think of her voice here, her accent, the way she almost touched her manicured finger to the corner of her painted lip when she spoke, Darling, I've got to go to Dubai! Yes, at the end of the month! What will the nanny do!

Then she turned to me and said smiling, Well, I suppose she'll get along. Then she said, Really I don't know how you manage with two. I could never do it, I'd be crawling up the walls! You must be so busy!

I nodded and smiled and said something about children. Running after them. Busy, yes, I was so busy. She said something else or nodded.

I really had to go look for E. I have to go look for E, I said, and M's boss's wife nodded, managing to look only very slightly relieved. I got up and pulled at the bottom of my dress, trying to unstick it from my back.

I walked down the hall. My feet were quiet on the gleaming parquet floor, the floor that was clean enough to eat caviar off, that was slick enough for dancing, that was made of hundreds of tiny pieces laid down one by one by someone else. I stuck my finger in my mouth and then touched a wall leaving a wet print. E, I called but not too loudly. There were so many doors. The bathroom is just down the hall, to the right, M's boss's wife called out from the living room.

I opened the first door in the hallway and found a bedroom. A guest room it must have been. More white walls. A bed with a plush dove-grey headboard and an opera sofa tucked under the window. The sofa had a curved back, soft, like the neck of a fallen giraffe. Like the neck of a giraffe that was lying down, shot on the Serengeti or some other place that wasn't here. There was a door inside the room and I stepped inside to open it saying, E? But not really meaning it. On the other side of the door was a bathroom with a freestanding tub deep enough, almost, to drown in standing up, but no E.

A line of unused soaps cut to look like amber were arranged on a shelf. The faucet rose up from the sink like a taxidermied bird, frozen in flight. I felt suddenly trapped in a flashing clean menagerie of fixtures and fittings. I stumbled back toward the door and managed to get out into the hall. The next door I tried was the kitchen, presided over by a green La Cornue stove with brass trim. Then, a closet with a maid's uniform hanging on a hook behind a door.

I really couldn't find her. I went back to the living room. M said, Did you find her? I said no and M looked to his boss, to his boss's wife and smiled at them and said something that was supposed to be about E that wasn't really about her. She's always this or that. When you're a guest in other people's houses, you have to say things to each other for them to hear. Oh E, we'd have to say, she's always like this, or this, whether she was or wasn't.

I sat back down at the occasional table. M's boss's wife looked up from the calendar on her phone and poured me another cup of tea. She offered me the plate of macaroons but by then I knew the game and said, No thank you, in the right sort of mildly shocked oh-I-couldn't-possibly sort of way.

I drank the tea and M's boss's wife sighed and tapped some more at her phone. There, she said, looking up. Tickets are booked, she said. Darling, she said, to M's boss, I'll be gone for a week. I'll miss you so much! And M's boss smiled back at her and patted the baby and it was clear that of course they would miss her too and also that they would love her so much more when she got back. Maybe he said it, M's boss, We'll love you so much more when you get back, he might have said. Well maybe they would.

There's always so much to do! she said and smiled and looked at me and what else could either of us have done with that. Yes, I said and crossed my legs the other way and smiled again and got up to look for E.

Finally I found her. She was in the hall bathroom, opening bottles of oil and soaps and pouring them down the sink. The room smelled so strongly of perfume that I took a step back then of course immediately ran inside and grabbed her arm.

What are you doing, I almost yelled, pulling her out of the bathroom. Too roughly, too roughly. I knew it was. I couldn't bend well in the dress. I couldn't grab her and run away like I should have in my stockinged feet that were already slipping. The floor seemed to have turned to ice underneath me, just like that.

She looked at me with her dark nothing eyes and all I could do was pull her out into the hall. My hands were shaking again and for a moment I wasn't pulling her anymore but holding on. I left her in the hallway and ran into the bathroom and shut the door. I opened the faucet and let the water run. I rinsed out all the little bottles that E had left in the bottom of the sink. They looked maybe like scarabs, lying there, spent. I lined them up on the little wooden shelf by the sink where E had surely found them, but that wasn't right. I turned the tap back on again, as high as it would go and I smashed the bottles one by one into the perfect porcelain finish of the sink. The bottles chipped the sink where they broke, throwing themselves against the finish like those pods of whales that kill themselves sometimes, hurling their great and perfect bodies up onto the beaches for nothing. Sometimes where they broke, the bottles, the two cut places touched each other for just a moment like veins, like anything at all that had been done could be undone, the doing of it. I crushed the bottles all back into sand and washed all the bits and pieces down the sink. I pulled all of the quilted tissues out of the tissue box and stuffed the toilet up with them. If anyone asked I would tell them E had done it.

One of the bottles I didn't break though, a small one, grey-green, about the size of my index finger with a red cut-glass top the size of a knuckle bone. I slipped it into the pocket of my dress. Hah! Because I had also been a child, because I was still capable of thoughtlessness, of recklessness, of a little bit of life. Inside the bottle it smelled like mist and moss clinging to some mountain rock. It smelled like the last tiny bit of morning.

I left the bathroom and collected E and we went back into the living room. There was light everywhere there, still in all the right places. We were washed in it as we came out from the hall. There they are, M said.

M's boss's wife was holding the baby, bouncing her a little against her shoulder, running her hand along her back, humming. They sort of blurred together, baby and mother, there where her lips and cheek touched the soft swoop of her mother's neck. They were like a paperclip, made of one long line. The simplest thing done exactly right.

M was standing at a window with M's boss, looking out over the lake. The afternoon was over. We made our excuses, said thank you thank you thank you and we'll have to do this again soon. Then we were through the door and out into the hall. B was slipped into his stroller asleep and didn't wake and while we climbed into the elevator smiling and waving back towards the door we looked every one of us like wonderful people and best families.

Don't forget to have the arrangements made for you, M's boss said. We've got to get out there Monday. I'll call Aurelie and let her know. She's going to have a hard time finding first-class tickets for both of us I think, but I imagine she'll work some magic for you. M laughed a bit. M was so good-natured. M knew just when to play along. M's boss said, All right then and winked at me. M's boss's wife said something to me about the children and made a nice face. I made my nice face then and wished her good luck on her trip and with the baby.

We were almost done. We were all horses coming round the final turn. Our sides steaming and bloody maybe but we could all see the finish line now. M shut us all up tight inside the birdcage elevator. We went creakily down, and then we were out again on the street.

13

M pushed the stroller down the sidewalk. B slept like a picture of a baby. The lake was so blue and beautiful and I put my arm around M's waist and E ran on ahead of us. I leaned into him a little, just testing really, a foot on a frozen lake in March. He looked down at me and smiled.

If only we could have been exactly like we must have looked to other people. If only we could be like pictures, all light-caught surface with nothing inside. All emptied out and perfect. M and I could hold hands every Saturday for a hundred years and always be the same. We could match each other step for step with nothing in between us, or perhaps we wouldn't move at all.

Across the street from us a young woman in a green dress put her hand up. I thought she might be hailing a cab but after a moment I realized she was looking at us. A tram slid between us and when it had passed, there she was, running across the street. She was tall, with long legs and long hair, so she got over to us quickly. She was so quick that she arrived in pieces, first her long long legs, then her hips, then all the rest of her. She was waving a phone at M.

Wait, a moment, she said a little breathlessly. I only just heard. Damn these shoes, she said, and put out a hand to steady herself on M's shoulder. She did this casually, her eyes on her shoes, her hand knew the height of him by heart. I felt the line of her zip down me suddenly, when she did that. Touched him. Zip. Right through me.

Damn these shoes, she said again, smiling. Teasing. A nice girl. She smiled nicely at everyone. M, me, everyone.

They're no good for running, she said. Jean should know not to call me with anything urgent on Saturday, when he knows I might be wearing these shoes, she said, still teasing.

She had the most delicious Parisienne accent. One of those accents that laps at the words like a cool tide, drawing everything around her closer, closer, closer.

I was on my way to Jean's she said. Just now. To check the arrangements. But then I saw you. She said this to M and she smiled at M.

Then, balanced only on the needle heel of one of her boots, she teetered, started to fall, came suddenly undone, and M reached out and caught her. It took my breath away when he did that. When he caught her like that. To see her a moment later saved, which in this case is to say in his arms. For that same moment I was underwater, plunged breathless into it. I mean, I couldn't breathe.

E was pulling my hand. I hadn't seen her come back. Really, I had forgotten all about her. Who's that lady, she said and M laughed with the woman still in his arms and the woman laughed with M's arms still around her. M tipped her back up and they untangled themselves. His hand caught in the strap of her tiny glittering bag and so for a moment there was a thin gold chain wrapped around them both.

This is Aurelie, M said. My assistant.

Aurelie.

!

I can't believe it! the woman who was Aurelie said, pushing a lock of hair from her eyes, pulling her dress back down across her thighs. She was testing the heels of her boots on the cobble-stones, putting herself back together. Playing at it.

This is why every French girl knows it is terrible luck to work weekends, she said, smiling at M. But these Swiss. What do they know.

M kept his hand under her elbow until she was steady, then let her go. You can get the tickets? he asked her and she said, Of course! I only wanted to know if you preferred the early flight or midday. Monsieur Jean, he likes to sleep in, but I thought perhaps you would like to go earlier.

No, M said after a moment. No, that's all right. We can go out midday together.

She nodded and pulled up her phone, checked something. Tap, tap, tap, went her manicured nails against the little screen.

Parfait, she said. Got it.

M sighed, tired. He was so tired and so important, there on the street. He was thinking maybe right now about some deal to be struck or renegotiated, he was thinking maybe right now about important things. All right, he said, I suppose I'll see you Monday then. You're coming with us?

Of course, she said, I wouldn't miss it. Well, have to run, she said. She had lots of work, there were tickets to book, a plane to catch. These Swiss, they never know how to stop working and have some fun, she said. I was watching M watch her. I was hearing all the things that she was saying right over the droning buzz that was starting up inside my ears.

She ran back across the street in her black heels, in her green dress, leaving us all standing, to me like dazed bystanders around a cavern, a wreckage, a sudden pillaging hole in the earth.

I pulled my shoulders up around me and tried to stop my thoughts before they happened, but I already knew that I knew. I knew that I knew that I knew and I knew that there was no stopping knowing. There was no stopping knowing at all.

Another tram pulled up and let off a stream of people and we were all swallowed up and suddenly a part of it all. All the people moving past us towards the lake took bits of us with them. Take it, I said.

There was a shop I wanted to go in, a shop I'd been wanting to go in for a while, for the guest room. For the white sheets. It was the best, maybe, in the whole city, for linens. It was right up the street. I told M, I'll only be a minute. I was starting to sweat. The store looked cool, almost dark inside. Come inside, it said, and see all our pretty things. We have what you need in here, it whispered. Price tags dangled in the window like loose teeth.

What, M said. In there?

Yes, I said. Yes. Yes. Yes.

Something was going to happen to me. Sweat, tears. Something. I was already reaching for the door handle. I had to keep going fast to stop my thoughts from coming, to keep ahead of them.

M hesitated. It looks a little cramped in there, he said. The stroller won't fit. Here, he said, and handed me his wallet. Here, take this. You stay. I'll take the kids back to the apartment. Take some time for yourself, he said. You're always with the kids, he said. You deserve a break. Have fun, he said. Have fun! I'll see you when you get back. He said that too.

My heart was going so fast. We can say so many words sometimes and never say a thing. If you close your eyes you could be anywhere and that is always true.

A tram came and he got on it, the number twelve. He pushed the stroller easily, held E easily with his other hand. They would be fine. He could even make them dinner. M had always been a good cook. A really surprisingly good one. Back when he was in grad school he used to make bread dough in the mornings and it would rise all day and make our apartment smell like yeast and honey.

Once he cooked us a steak that cost him as much as I made in a whole day and we ate it sitting on the back porch off paper plates balanced on our knees. Once we went camping and forgot our tent. Once he bought me a book that was just exactly the one I wanted and I thought that no one could have known that I would have loved just exactly that one but me. Once he had a green car that I had to push down the block to get started and then run around to the passenger side and jump in before he put it in gear. Once he asked his grandmother to teach him to sew and he sewed me a shirt and I wore it, even though it was terribly made and much too large for me, for months, until one of the sleeves actually fell off while I was at work. All these things were true about him. All these things were true about me too.

I was alone on the street in front of the shop. I felt naked and out of place without a stroller in front of me. It was as if there was nothing left to explain me, nothing left to help make sense of me at all. I almost ran after M, after the tram, but that would have been silly and I've always, to be honest, had a horror of creating a scene, so it seemed that the only thing to do was to go inside the shop. Sometimes we're just left aren't we? Sometimes the only thing to do is the thing we said we would.

It was an old shop that sold linens, the best. Hydrocotton double-weave towels from Denmark. Tablecloths, tablesquares and runners from Ekelund. It was the kind of place where the shop girl might ask you whether you preferred to sleep on sheets made from French, or Belgian, flax. I really had been meaning to go for some time. Everything that I had said to M had been true.

I went straight to the bed linens and touched them. I put my hands all over them. I slipped my fingers in between the folded stacks of them. A shop girl came over and began telling me the names of each kind of sheet, explaining to me the different washes. Stone wash to save the colour, vintage wash for sheets that never aged, cotton wash for soft and bright and new. Then she started to show me the possible colours, lifting up the folded sheets one by one and holding up a corner, to show me how they, each differently, caught the light.

Ocean Smoke, she said, over a soft grey bundle. Dawn Owl, she said holding up another in blue. Mole's Back, she hummed over a mushroom-brown set. Her voice sounded very close to an incantation. Reverent maybe, and why not? What is a name but a spell to bring something into life and keep it there? A dressmaker's pin slipped through the shoulders, isn't it? A name. It holds you in place, makes you real.

Isn't that why mothers name their babies really. With these sounds, these particular sounds, don't they say, the new mothers, I will keep you alive and here with me. Like I said, dressmakers. Pins.

Tallow, the girl said holding up a wan yellow sheet.

Elephant Tusk, holding up ivory coloured shams.

Elephant's Breath, holding a slightly darker one.

The sheets I guess broke everything down into pieces. Carcasses snipped up into their most lovely parts.

Do you prefer the Tusk, madam? the shop girl said, watching me in that careful way of well-trained shop girls. Or the Breath? They are both so lovely, she said.

And they were, they really really were.

Approximately four billion years from now our galaxy is going to crash into our nearest neighbour, the Andromeda galaxy, and a new galaxy is going to form. Someone some- where has already given that new galaxy a name. Milkomeda. Imagine the audacity of that. The ridiculous human-ness of that. To look four billion years into the future, into a future in which it is almost inconceivable that any human will be alive, and to begin to name things. Just how far removed though is a galaxy from a child? What is a child but two strands of data ploughing into each other in the dark cosmos of a woman's body. Galaxies, don't they crash together every day.

How could anyone sleep on sheets dyed a colour called Elephant Tusk? Beauty makes the unimaginable easy though, and the sheets were that.

I pointed to the whitest white and bought them. The set at the top of the stack. Don't tell me anything about it, I said to the shop girl. I bought the whole set, duvet cover, pillow- cases, shams with pressed edges, fitted sheets and flat.

The girl told me about the sheets anyway, she couldn't be stopped. She told me how they were made from cotton that was brought to Italy from Egypt and woven there on giant hundred-year-old looms where the sun streamed endlessly through farmhouse windows and every grandmother made raviolis that were tiny and soft like babies' finger bones. You paid extra but you could feel the sun, the way it had soaked into the strands, the warp and weave of the cloth. You paid extra but you dreamed every night of wheat fields and olive trees and rolling hills, sun on your shoulders and tables dripping with olive oil and prosciutto. She could have been telling me that, I was trying desperately not to pay attention. She wrapped the sheets in yards and yards and yards of tissue, everything was encased when she was done. Encased just exactly so.

I bought a throw pillow too to put on top of the bed when no one was in it. I said don't tell me anything about it, but she did anyway. She talked and talked and so I had to talk too. It had been painted, she told me, in Venice. And I said, hesitating, that it looked just like it had. She thought I meant something about the colour. Oh yes, she said, that blue, it only comes from, but I wasn't listening. I meant only that it looked like a beautiful thing that had already resigned itself to sinking into the sea and I loved it for that. In the painting on the pillow manic streaks of colour glubbed deeper and deeper underneath what was absolutely a beautiful and striking blue. Exuberance of the Resigned I would have called it, the colour, if it had been mine to name.

In a room behind the counter where the girl was slipping the last of my sheets into an embossed paper bag, I saw what I had really come for. Wooden shelves stacked high with duvets. Down, wool, bamboo, cotton, summer weights and winter weights, and, I had heard, read I mean, real eiderdowns. There was a skylight in the roof and as I walked into the room I saw how the light just tumbled down from it in strands like Rapunzel's hair, turning the duvets stacked on the shelves there a kind of gold. For a moment it was so quiet and wonderful inside me.

I asked the girl, who had of course followed me, to show me the eiderdowns. She pulled one down and unzipped it from its white cloth case and inside I saw what I had been looking for. I'll take it, I said, wanting to get out of the store now. Wanting to get it home, back to my room in the apartment. When shopping is done for me, it's done.

She tried to tell me a bit about the eider ducks, whose feathers were sewn into the duvet I had just purchased. She tried to tell me about the men and women in Iceland who collect their feathers, the feathers the eider ducks have used to line their nests. But I didn't want to hear her talk about it. I was here for my own purposes.

How could she know really anything important about the ducks, about me, about the sheets? How could she know, really know anything about the feathers that were sewn, hand-sewn by old Danish men in wool caps, into the feather-cloud pockets of the eiderdown. She didn't know that they weren't just any feathers wrenched off any old eider duck. She didn't know that the feathers I was purchasing were the feathers that the eider duck mothers make their nests with, only those. She was much too young to understand that the mother eider duck rips her warmest, her softest feathers from her own breast in order to make nests with them, the feathers, for her eggs. The girl was much too young to understand that these feathers were the only thing warm enough, soft enough, right enough to keep a mother eider duck's eggs alive in the freezing dead nothing northern winds of Iceland. The only thing. I wanted to laugh when I saw the eiderdowns stacked up in the room in the back of the shop because what comfort in this world is not made from the bodies of mothers. Their actual bodies.

After the babies hatch though, after they can fly, they have no more use for the nests. They leave and they leave the nests abandoned. As they should! As nature demands them to! After they leave, the feathers are left behind of course and rightly like garbage, like juice boxes, like yogurt tubs, like any other kind of trash.

More and More and More and More and Always February

Oh you clean here too? Not just up in the rooms? But isn't it the middle of the night? It's so hard to keep track of time when, well, when I'm down here. There aren't any windows down here. But of course you can see that. I'm just going to go back to sleep now, if that's all right with you. It's just that, well, these treatments make me so tired. It's the drugs maybe. I didn't know that. That you cleaned down here. I'm sorry, I think I threw up somewhere. I'm sorry about that.

Do you know she didn't come back? The woman with the ugly daughter? She never came back from the dentist. And I've been asking where she is. I've been asking and asking and asking but no one is hearing me. No one is hearing me at all.

Could you tell one of the guards to bring me some water? Sometimes they will. I'm so thirsty.

14

I stopped for a coffee inside one of the department stores on the Rue de Rive. I piled my bags up on the chair opposite me as if they were someone I could talk to. Quack, I could have whispered to my bags if I hadn't been in such a fancy place. I watched a woman with short ice-blonde hair slicked back from her face eat oysters at the bar. The man with her had poured her a glass of champagne but she wasn't touching it. She wasn't touching him either. Just the oysters. She slipped them one by one down her throat. Once or twice she checked the time on a rose-gold watch barnacled all over with diamonds that peeked out from the arm of her smart blue blazer.

I thought then, watching her, of something funny and smart to say about her and I wanted to tell M the thing that I had thought of. I wanted him to see her too, and I wanted him to see me. Me here and her. The woman with the gold watch and man she wasn't touching. Of course M wasn't there though and I had only my bags to talk to. Tant pis, I could have said, just then, and halfway I could have meant it.

We used to go to a particular restaurant, M and me, for celebrations, which at the time was another way to say Friday night. We only had enough money for two drinks per celebration. So we only got one each, one drink. The trick was to make the one drink last long enough for both of us to eat our fill of the free snacks, peanuts and olives and some kind of spicy cracker, so we wouldn't be starving in the morning. The trick was to do this but to be not obvious about it.

These little things got lost so easily when there was no one to snatch them up with. The lady with the oysters for example, would be lost, was being lost right now, as I watched her. I can be funny and I can be a good time I told the bags in front of me, but quietly and with my mouth mostly hidden by my coffee cup so I wouldn't be seen talking to my shopping.

A woman with a little dog under her arm hit the back of my chair with her purse and I slurped my coffee. One big gulp down the hatch. I looked up then across the street, and saw Nell, walking arm in arm with the man I had seen in the park. It was just the two of them. Couples have a certain way of walking, when they have children but their children aren't with them. Well they do, and they were walking like that. In that way. She was laughing with her head tilted back, open-mouthed. Just as I watched, she almost stepped in something. I couldn't see what, and he picked her up, actually picked her all the way up in the air and lifted her away from it, whatever it was. Saving, maybe, maybe probably, her shoes from something terrible and awful and unmentionable on the street.

She looked at me. For the second that she was up in the air, her eyes flew across the street, across the tops of the heads of all the people, through the glass windows of the cafe, past the woman with ice-blonde hair who was still not touching the man she was with, all the way to me. Zip. A little spark. We knew who we were.

I grabbed the bags and ran out of the cafe after her. I can't explain it. She wasn't asking me to follow her. I bumped into a couple as I ran out. It seemed for a moment that everyone was intertwined and between all the linked arms and hands holding on to one another that I would never be able to get away. Smiles usually work in those sorts of situations though and I took out one of my best and apologized to the man for knocking the hat out of his hand with all the bags in mine and I was free.

I arrived out on the street shaking, heaving under all my bags, looking for her. I was like a bride. I had that many yards of white fabric piled up around me. I thought I had lost her, that I hadn't been quick enough and I really thought of screaming. I stamped my foot a little and the pigeons ruffled and fussed but then I saw her, heading towards the lake, and I ran off in a burst and flurry.

She didn't want me to follow her. I could see that. She looked over her shoulder once, and saw me chasing after her and she frowned but I kept following. I can't say what I meant to do. She was wearing a dress that should have showed her shoulders but she had a heavy scarf draped over them, one you couldn't see through even if you tried. He had an arm around her waist. I couldn't seem to catch up to them even though I was almost running. Almost but not quite.

They were hard to keep track of. Crowds of strollers kept swarming over them and spitting them back out in improbable places. One minute they would be walking past one of the lakeside bars and the next they would be kissing under a tree in the Jardin Anglais. It was one of those days when everyone was kissing so even then they were hard to pick out. Only her dark wool scarf gave them away.

More and more people kept pouring down the promenades towards the lake. The benches were filled with tanned legs all tangled up together. Aurelie's legs maybe, touching M's. Eating oysters one after the other. Neither one of them would have checked their watch. Oh, she would have said, and she would have tossed her hair and been absolutely transfixing doing it, saying only oh and slurping oysters. All this was possible and possibly true. I slammed my bags hard into the side of a small but intricately decorated fountain and the water reared up and splashed me and I looked down at my side for E to blame it on, Look! I could yell. It's a game, this business of banging and splashing! But of course she wasn't there, E wasn't, and everything was real and awful and I looked all soft and round and spilling.

I was going to apologize to the people sitting at the foot of the fountain, the people, hundreds and hundreds of them, or maybe only two, who had been kissing and who were now staring at me, drenched. But then I caught sight of Nell and I laughed, Ha! All sharp and purposeful, because I had someone to run after, somewhere to go.

Aurelie's legs though, they had been so long, so thin and long, like she was one long line drawn flippantly and gorgeously all at once and here I was so pulpy, so hot and scribbled and stumbling.

People lounged closer and closer to one another at the cafe tables as I passed them, chasing Nell now through the park. Fingers pressed other fingers, the sides of tanned feet touched the sides of other tanned feet. It was summer and lips drank from the same bottles. Shades of lipstick piled up on top of each other on the sides of glasses. Red and pink and red again. Men over-tipped and women finished each other's drinks. The swans in the lake gobbled up the bread that was thrown to them, gorging on soggy crusts, on the occasional croissant. Men dropped their hands lower down the backs of women. Women ran their fingers over their collarbones and touched the corners of their eyes. The day was so warm, warm all the way through and everyone knew it. Knew that on an afternoon like this one, hands were free to wander where they liked.

I spotted Nell heading for the taxi-boat dock and ran after her. We waited in line, me two steps behind her pretending like this was all possibly a coincidence. Her tucking her shoulder into the man a bit. Her pretending that I wasn't there. Well and wasn't this just so explainable? Weren't we just neighbours heading home after a stroll in the park? Didn't we both have to cross back over the lake? How could any of this really have been otherwise? Nell could have glanced at me there so close behind her but she didn't. Oh, hi, she could have said, I know you from the park. Her hair looked dull, I could see this now, looking at her from behind. She was smiling up at the man above her but her hair looked like it was some dead thing hanging down her back.

We were the first ones on the boat when it pulled up. Nell and the man headed for the prow, taking the seats where the spray from the lake would touch their faces. I took a seat inside with my bags. More people began filling up the boat behind me. We were all heading across the water towards another garden. The one with the reflecting pools and the stone mansion with the blue shutters that was always mobbed with people and yet looked always also, so all by itself.

Someone made their way past me. A woman in a green dress, a dress that was impossibly just exactly like the dress I had so recently seen wrapped around Aurelie. Wrapped around Aurelie when she was wrapped in M's arms. I shut my eyes blink, and cut her out, but she was still there when I opened them again. I pinched my arms too but she didn't go away. Another women in a green dress passed me, her hem just skirting my knees as she made her way towards the prow. A woman in a green dress sat down next to me. I angled my knees slightly away from her. A woman in a green dress sat down on my other side. The boat was filling up with women in green dresses.

I grabbed up my shopping bags and clutched them on my lap like children. There was the scent of almonds in the air. I smelled it when the women moved, as if their dresses were lined with almonds, or they all had almonds tucked behind their ears, or folded up behind their knees. The captain blew the whistle and the boat pushed off into the lake. The women in the green dresses ignored me but when I breathed in, they leaned towards me and when I breathed out they leaned away. I couldn't see Nell behind all the fluttering green silk, behind all the crossed ankles and needle black heels. I couldn't see her. I wasn't even sure anymore whether she was really there. I can be so much fun at parties, I wanted to shout to the women, but I held on to my shopping bags and shut my eyes and pretended I had a headache, as if the sun were too bright then, to me, where I was sitting.

One of the women, the woman to my right, who wore a green dress that ended just above her ankles, reached down into one of my shopping bags and touched the top of one of my tissue-wrapped parcels with her green painted fingernails. She didn't look at me. She never looked at me once.

When the boat docked I leapt up and began pushing past the women, past all their slippery silk-covered knees. I held my bags close to me so they wouldn't tangle in all the long hair that poured in wavy locks down from the tops of their heads. I bent this way and that to avoid all the long fingers and manicured nails. I almost couldn't breathe for the smell of almonds. They watched me. They smiled pretty smiles. They exhaled their pretty almond breath. Perhaps I was faster than they were. Perhaps I was fast enough. The captain held out a hand to help me off the boat but I didn't have one to give. I was all tangled up in my bags. Instead, I heaved myself back on solid ground and ran for home.

The garden where the boat had docked, the Jardin de Mon Repos, was filling with more and more women in green dresses. They poured in like locusts, the kind that strip whole villages down to their posts and their bones. Shoulder to shoulder, they jostled for space on the walking paths, they overflowed the benches. In the Musée d'Histoire des Sciences, I could see them peering out of each one of the windows, some held tiny pairs of binoculars up to their eyes.

They ate ice cream from glass dishes at the vine-covered tables of the restaurant La Perle du Lac. They licked their spoons. They scraped the bottoms of the dishes. Waiters in green dresses weaved in among the tables carrying trays of espresso and pastis. One of the waiters dropped her tray and the women at the surrounding tables pounced on her like jackals, putting her tray back together or ripping her apart.

At the Jardin Botanique women in green dresses filled the glass greenhouses. They steamed up the panelling with their almond breath. Some women in green dresses were planting flowers and more women in green dresses hung high up in the trees like unripe fruit, motionless, except for some that checked their phones.

The reflecting pools were clogged with women in green dresses floating mildly on their backs and other women in green dresses stood at the sides of the pools holding long-handled nets, trying to fish them out. At the Place des Nations, women in green dresses ran back and forth in the fountain, laughing as the shooting jets of water rained down on them, plastering their backs with dark green silk. Women in green dresses climbed the statues and sat sunning themselves demurely on the concrete benches, their hands resting beautifully just beneath their throats.

I ran out to the street, which is to say I ran almost into it, right as the number fifteen tram pulled up to the stop. The driver bleated his horn at me and I fell back onto the platform gasping. I turned back to the fountains but found them empty, the women in green dresses had vanished or become leaves, hanging so lush and green and glinting from all the cernuous trees. My breath was ragged and a man asked me if I was all right and I had the urge to, really suddenly found I almost couldn't not, spit at him, my mouth pooled with drool and murk, but I only smiled and nodded and wiped savagely at the corners of my lips. I grabbed up all my bags and hurried away from the park almost running for the station where I could catch a tram that would take me back to the apartment.

A couple of women in green dresses hid sulkily behind the dingy apartment windows overlooking the street. Further down, toward the lake a woman in a green dress pushed a cleaning trolley in front of her but no one seemed to notice. It seemed possible that my eyes had specks in them or were haunted.

I ran through the train station when I got there, following carefully the raised track in the centre of the floor that is laid down in order to get blind people from one place to another. The track that is only wide enough for a single foot. A man stepped across the track in front of me and I almost reached out and pushed him. He saw my face, the way I was pulling it, or maybe the way I jerked suddenly towards him, and I knew that if he had fallen then, I would have thrown myself on top of him and eaten him up. That I would have scratched at his smooth skin until there was blood beneath my nails.

What I'm trying to say is that I was suddenly boiling, that it was almost like the ground might split and melt beneath my feet. A woman in a green dress crept out of the corner of my eye and I thought, Got you! But it was only nothing and there was no one there and I thought of that fine gold chain winding around Aurelie, winding around M. I thought about her, Aurelie, who was the type of woman who could leave her house with only such a delicate purse and all my shopping bags turned to so much cumbersome ash in my swollen hands. There was something in that chain, in the fineness of it, in its

184

dainty winking effervescence, that I could never buy or pretend to have for even just an afternoon.

I got to the end of the little path and left the train station and found my place at the tram stop and thought, There, I'm through it. I waited in line and bought my ticket, counting out the change just right and feeding the coins into the machine one by one. I was proceeding calmly, putting in the coins and collecting my ticket and standing with the other people who were waiting for the tram.

The tram came and I got on it, and other people got on with me, just pouring onto it like water or krill or like garbage. There was a single woman in a green dress on the tram, and she stepped backwards towards me, dripping her long hair down inside and all across my delicately wrapped eiderdown and I reached out and pulled her hair hard, hard enough to yank back her long neck. The woman screamed and put her hand up to her hair and I admit that shocked me but I waited and nobody had seen who had done it. We were so many arms you see, in the crowd. I buried my hands in all my shopping and cast around, with all the other passengers, my most innocent looks. The woman started to cry, reaching around and holding the back of her head, almost cradling it, but she didn't turn to see me.

When the tram pulled up at my stop I ran all the way to the front door of the apartment, fast with my eyes almost closed, feeling better and better the tighter I shut them.

The door wasn't locked, but I locked it behind me after I was inside. Lock, deadbolt, chain. Click, slam, slide. Everything felt instantly better. When kids played tag in the Parc des Délices, older kids, not mine, they called the place where they were safe, the spot where they couldn't be gotten, the maison magique, and what could have been more right than that.

It is the most wonderful thing really, to have a door, a personal door that is all your own, that you can shut on everything else. Of course all the real true magic is in locks, wood panelling and hinges.

I found M playing a game in the living room with E. He held B, sleeping, gurgling and coo-dreaming in the crook of his arm. I walked past them with my bags and he laughed and said, Well, I see you found what you were looking for. I smiled and curtseyed a little with the bags, playing, playful, fun. Just a little shopping, I said. I set the bags down in the guest room and closed the door.

M and I went to Paris for our honeymoon. We spent all our money on the plane tickets and hadn't planned a thing beforehand, so we found ourselves stuck in a hostel in a really terrible part of town. M in the men's dorms, me in the women's. For seven nights we slept on plastic mattresses, listening to the snores of other people, their bouts of night-time itchiness, their French cheese farts. It was, I swear to god, the most romantic thing.

We'd meet each morning at breakfast and kiss over juice-machine apple juice, watery butter packets and limp croissants. I would sit on the same side of the table as him and we would look out at all the other people paying fifteen euros a night for the privilege of being in Paris. For being right there where we were. I would lean into his shoulder and press my face into his old college hoodie that smelled of chemical detergent and other people's socks and he would jump up and get me another cup of push-button coffee if I asked him, anytime I asked him to.

For a week we walked up one street and down another. We shared baguettes. We marvelled at enormous doors. When it rained we walked along the Seine because that way we had the whole river to ourselves. We went to museums but they hardly mattered. Nothing in them was alive like we were alive. In the Louvre a tour group took a picture of us kissing in front of the Venus de Milo. What I'm trying to say is, we didn't even know the statue was there.

M lost his wedding ring in Paris. It was a half-size too big and it slipped off his finger while we ran through the Gare de Lyon trying to catch the late-night train back to the hostel. We discovered his empty finger just as we took our seats. Just behind us though, a woman, yelling at a station attendant as she boarded the train, pushed a small child through the closing doors and squeezed in afterwards herself. This child was playing with the ring. M's lost one. She was flipping it between her fingers and when she dropped it we snatched it up while the mother, who we were afraid of because of the way she had been yelling, wasn't looking. The child only stared at us. We hopped off the train at our stop and ran all the way back to the hostel. We had it back, the ring, and it never slipped again. After that, losing it and finding it again, it was the perfect size. M thought maybe he'd made a mistake, maybe the child hadn't been playing with his ring at all, but how could we have been wrong? How would it have been possible for us to steal something? We who were so in love. Paris is for lovers and everything in Paris belonged to us. What could have been more true than that?

After Paris, after the ring, I've always had a suspicion about losing things. It seems lucky somehow to do it. It seems like the lost thing or things will come back better than before, a more perfect fit. At least there's the possibility of that. Miracles can only happen to people who have lost things. My mother used to say that to me and it seems very much the truth. It's also maybe true that we can never really lose the things we love. Our love makes them belong only to us and so we can smile and not ever worry. We expect miracles! We who are deserving people. We lovers who love who we love.

M was getting up off the floor, smiling at me. He was such a good father. E was tending to the baby giraffe again who was sick and looking for its mother. She's gone, E kept telling it and waiting, looking at it closely as if to check for any expression that might run across its face. M set B down in his crib. Shh, he whispered to me, don't wake him. I only just got him to sleep.

M had to go to the office. Only for an hour, maybe two,

he said. Aurelie and Jean wanted to finalize arrangements. He kissed me before I could say, Stop. Before I could say, Don't go. I'll make dinner just the way you like. I'll say the thing that you will love, the thing that will make you laugh, the thing that will make you stay.

We used to eat sandwiches together every Wednesday night and drink lemonade and we would laugh at ourselves because it felt then that being an adult could still be just pretending, a coat we could take on and off.

I made noodles for E and we slurped them up one by one like snakes and then we all went to bed together, E and B and I. B nursed all night long but I didn't mind. I rocked him from one side to the other. The hours were things inside of things inside of other things. All packed away together. We all kept time like this, inside ourselves.

M didn't come home from the office that night, but that was all right because in the morning he was there. I woke up late and found him. He'd already made coffee. It was on the table waiting for me. Sorry about last night, he said. One of the computers crashed, he said. I imagined the data spilling out like oil, little bits and big bits of the company's money spreading out thick and dark all over the office carpet, sinking into it.

He and Jean had been scrambling all night, M said, to fix it. I could see them working in the dark like fishermen in the frozen north, passing all the hours hauling in nets, the water so cold and dripping like nectar off the almost frozen bodies of their silvery catch. Work work work, M said, grinning at me in that way that I really loved. He had the handle of his rolling suitcase in his hand and I was only just seeing that.

It should only be for a few weeks, he was saying. Jean and I decided to leave today, get a good night's sleep before the meetings and all that. Besides, the flights are better today, would you believe it? Aurelie could only get us coach on Monday and, but he stopped talking when he saw my face. When he saw something or other in it, in the lines of it, the lines around my mouth and eyes, or maybe it was the way I held my hands or maybe it was something else, but anyway he stopped. Then he said more softly, in his I'm-actually-really-and-truly-really-sorry voice, There's no way to avoid it. He had to talk to some other men or women who owned or ran some other businesses in some other place or places. He really had to, he said. He wished he didn't, he said, but Jean needed him. The company did. Conversations had to be had, handshakes and cards exchanged with those other men, those other women. Important people talking to other important people. Wine and lunch and decisions. Hotel lobbies, pressed suits and the right kind of laughing.

It's not what you think, he said. These trips, they're just meetings, they're always so boring, they always run on and on, people saying the same things, telling the same awful jokes. It's not all glamour, he laughed, and I laughed too. Poor you, I said, of course it isn't glamorous, of course it's work.

Of course I was only picturing the cool white of the hotel sheets, the sheets that were tucked and fluffed and made right every day by a horde of efficient maids, the places that were clean without me cleaning them, the food that was there without me making it, the guests that clinked their rings against their glasses and ordered another round at midnight just for fun, and for being alive and because everything was constantly being taken care of, of course I was only picturing these things because I didn't understand, how could I, what it was all about.

Of course I was also thinking of Aurelie, who would be there, who would be flying with him maybe with nothing to hold her back or down but her tiny gold-chained purse. She could have packed a hundred dresses in her tiny purse, they were so fine, the silk so delicate and sheer as to be almost only a trick of the light.

M walked into E's bedroom and ran his hands through her hair while she slept. He told me he'd miss us. I said good luck and I really meant it. I said that E and B would miss him too. I told him that they loved him, that they were really lucky to have a father like him. I said that we would all be here for him when he got back. I said that we loved him, that we loved him very much and every day.

What else could I have said? I was almost chasing him down the hallway, saying this, saying that. He kissed the top of my head and I was suddenly so small and I was sinking and sinking into the carpet. He gave me dates and places,

I'm going first here, he said, for this many days, and then I'm going here for this other number of days and nights, and then, he said there will be another place, and he listed more days and nights but I was too far away to hear him. I was floating off into another place even with him holding me there by the shoulders, kissing my cheek. We had a party, I wanted to tell him, we had a party and we left the door open all night, and I, and you, and after we, and afterwards it was all so and also. He kissed me but it wasn't me, I wasn't even there. He left and the whole apartment smelled like him for a moment and then it didn't because he was gone.

March

Hark hark the dogs do bark.
The beggars are coming to town.
Some in rags and some in jags.
And one in a velvet gown.

Do you know that one?

Do you know it's my birthday? Soon? Or maybe today? Or maybe it was yesterday? I never used to tell anyone that it was my birthday. Didn't want to make a fuss. Well, look how that turned out. So Happy Birthday to me! Yes! Saturday's child works hard for a living. I say, works hard at living. And I do! I've stacked all my troubles up in a heap and run at it.

Listen, I wanted to tell you, I'm sorry for, well, down there, in the basement. The other day, or the other night, whichever it was. I made such a mess didn't I! Sometimes I can't stop myself from doing that, after the treatments or sometimes if

I think the wrong thought, sometimes we all just turn into meat don't we? Become a body I mean. Sometimes we're brought up against exactly what we are. But if I say, Désolée pour tout à l'heure, can we still call ourselves friends?

Do you know what that means? Literally? It means I'm sorry for everything in the hour. Or, I'm sorry for all the hours. Or, I'm sorry for everything that came before. Or, I'm sorry for everything and all the hours. I don't know. I don't speak French! I wish I did. I can only tell you what it could mean, what it possibly could, and I am! I am sorry! For all of the above. For all of it!

I would give you a present, if I had anything, to go with the sorry-saying. Something sweet. It seems like the right moment for chocolates. I would give you one of those little boxes that only come with two chocolates inside and a big ribbon to show the cost. I would give you the box and say, I was unbelievable! And you would laugh and say, You're always unbelievable. And I would feel so relieved because I would know that you knew that I didn't mean it.

Then we would share them. We would have one each and we would say, Aren't we being naughty! And we would say, Look at us! And we would say, Thank goodness for Winter Coats! And we would pretend that it would never be July.

Honestly, I wish we were friends! You can't know how much I wish that. I wish that we would sit down somewhere for coffee. Then, when we were done, I would get up and take your purse once maybe by mistake. We would laugh about this because of how similar our purses looked, and we'd laugh again and we would say, We never noticed that before! How could we have not! And we would trade back purses and smile and wave and promise to see each other soon. We don't see enough of each other! you would say to me, when we were leaving. I feel sure that you would say that.

They tell me I'll have my hair washed soon. And brushed. Just like before. I hope that means that she'll come back, the lady who cut my hair. I haven't seen her and my hair is really starting to pull itself into the most awful mess. Of course you can see that. But you haven't mentioned it. I can see that you're not the type of person who would mention a thing like that. I try to wash it in the showers but of course they're not showers really are they? They're just giant spigots of icy water that they dunk me in twice a week. I see that it's important, I understand that, cleanliness is next to . . . I'm not asking for anything about it to be changed but certainly it's no place for a lady to brush her hair. Anyways I only have my fingers and what really can I do with those.

If you see her ever, the lady who cut my hair, could you tell her, could you make sure that she knows that visiting hours are from two to four? Sometimes I go up to the window and shout that, with my face pressed right up to the glass. Sometimes I shout until my throat gets sore and I claw my arms with my fingernails. Visiting hours are from two to four! Sometimes it's just nice to have something to yell, isn't it? To have words to put to the sounds that want to come out of your throat.

She's not a visitor. I know that she's not. I don't want you to think that I'm confused on that point. So the visiting hours don't apply. I know that. It's just that I think it would be nice really, if she would come then, during visiting hours. If she would come specifically then to brush my hair and really, it seemed that she would care to know if there was a thing that I wanted. If there was a thing that I preferred. Really it seems as if she would care to know that.

It seems as if you would care to know that too. So, please, I know you're not supposed to say, that you're not supposed to talk to me about any of the others here but please. That woman, in the bed under the window. She never came back. You know she didn't. Please. I really have to know. Did they fix her teeth and did she start to talk and was everything fine and wonderful for her after that? That's possible. I know that's possible. For that to have happened. It's almost always possible for things to be fine and wonderful isn't it?

It's true that we're all disappearing, everyone in the world is I mean. Only here, it seems to be happening more quickly.

Everyone is gone all the time. Everyone is going down the drain. Only I'm stuck here waiting. I'm a bone aren't I? Caught in a dog's throat.

It's so dark here at night. It's so quiet without her snoring that my ears ring. When I'm alone and it's dark and the silence heaps up around me. When it puts its mouth to my ear and shrieks. Please. Just tell me where she went. I feel sure that that would help me. I feel so sure of it.

*   *   *

I had a little husband no bigger than my thumb,
I put him in a pint pot and there I bid him drum;
I bought a little handkerchief to wipe his little nose,
and a pair of little garters to tie his little hose.

What about that one? Do you know it? It's funny you know, the songs that get stuck, running and running through our heads.

What is the thing you are not saying. That's all they say to me now, there in their offices I mean. What is the thing. What is the thing. What is it. Sometimes I'm listening, sometimes I'm not, but they're still saying it. All the time they are. Sometimes I'm sitting in a chair, or sometimes I'm lying down. Sometimes it's one doctor. Sometimes it's two. Sometimes the men are doctors. Sometimes they're not. Sometimes I mean to say I'm lying down and they're not doctors, the men. I'm sure they're not.

We're running out of time, they say. That's my lawyer, who mainly says that. But there's too much time here anyway. So how could that concern me? It would be lovely to run out of it. I try to explain that to him but I don't think he sees what I mean.

He's such a funny man, I wish you could meet him. He always looks so tired, so, I don't know, briefcased. So be-biroed, so be-foldered and be-noted and be-cased. He has everything already printed out in triplicate when he gets here and he looks so tired, really so almost at the end of his rope that I want to tell him to take a seat even when he's already sitting down. Sometimes I want to lean over the table and kiss him right on his chapped lips and I have to quickly quickly quickly imagine myself as a toad to stop myself. I have to imagine my big toad's mouth and bulging swamp-water eyes. He says we have to concentrate on my case but I just blink my froggy eyes at him and flick my tongue. Visiting hours are from two to four I say sometimes because that's the only thing I can think of. I only say it because I'm trying to help, because I want to make him happy. I want him to tell me that's it, that's right, that's exactly right. Only I never do get it exactly right and usually we just sit there staring at each other across the table until I start cawing or shouting and I have to be taken away.

That's usually how it goes when he comes. I'm afraid I'm not much help to him at all.

It's important today, though, the visiting hours because he, my lawyer, said I might be getting a visitor today, after lunch. I'm going to be taken down to the waiting room, to well, wait I suppose. I can't tell you how wonderful it feels to know that. I wish the lady was here to brush out my hair but we mustn't be silly must we?

There are supposed to be rolls with lunch today. The soft kind with the dusting of flour on the top that looks like powdered sugar or snow. What's more is, they're my favourite, so today really must be lucky, today really must be all for me. We only get them sometimes, the rolls, not often at all, and do you know, I think that's nice. It gives me so much to look forward to. Really so much. I was shocked you know when I first got here and saw the food we were expected to eat, really shocked, but now, well, it's easy to see how nice the rest of it makes the rolls seem, don't you think? It's important to remember all the good things we have isn't it, to wear them like rings on our fingers? Not to forget a single good thing or we might lose it. It's possible to lose things that way, if we forget them. If we don't hold the thought of them all the time very very close to us. So, maybe a visitor, maybe a soft roll, maybe a bird at the window if I'm quiet and watchful.

It might be better if you left now. You see, I've got to get ready. We're both busy girls today.

*   *   *

Oh, it's you. Could you pass me a glass of water? I'd get up, I meant to get up, hours ago. Only I'm just so tired right now. So tired I could fall right through the sheets.

I think I might go back to sleep now, but if you leave a glass of water on the table, I'll know it was you that left it when I wake up.

When I wake up properly I mean, and am myself again, I'll know that, that it was you that left the glass.

It's just that right now I'm kind of carrying everything, all the shopping I mean, all the little things, and I can't move, and I just wish, really wish it would all push me into the ground. See I'm thin now and my shoulder blades could dig out the dirt underneath me like shovels, it could all just push me under right now, like that.

Why don't you go and leave me alone. I'm too tired just now. It's all just right now in front of me and I can't play or be solicitous.

*   *   *

A carrion crow sat on an oak.

Do you know that one? I hope you don't, it's terrible. Isn't it a pity? It's always the terrible things we can't forget.

Visiting hours are two to four. See? I wrote that down, in my new journal. Do you like it? It was a present from the doctors.

They tell me I'm supposed to write things down. They say they want to help me but I have to help them first. They tell me that I should try to write things down if I can't talk about them. It's a tool you see, like the sticks that those monkeys stick down into ant hills, only it's larger and has a pink cover.

But see? All I can write today is, Visiting hours are two to four. I suppose it's because I'm trying to write down the truth and that's as far as I can get.

Besides, I feel so calm today. Isn't it a wonderful thing to sit calmly and perfectly still? I'm like a little white boat on a blue lake. Why rake it all up? All that mess? Why try to get at it? When I can keep my head above the water like this, when I can sit so still like this and let the minutes wash over me like a tide.

Maybe in the spring, I said. Maybe I could write then, when the trees start to bud, when they start to get on with things.

When the birds come back, I can start by naming them one by one by one. In my diary I mean. Maybe I could scratch out the names of all the things that are getting on with it. Or maybe, then, I could write in my diary like a girl. The letters all soft bends and bounces. Maybe it all amounts to the same thing.

See? I have been given a list of prompts. I'm to answer them one by one until I find myself answering the questions that they want me to. Until the words I give them are the words they want. You see, I see how it goes. How they are playful maybe, or at least how they are playing a game with me. Anyway, I'm to give it to them at my next appointment and me wishing myself out of it doesn't change anything a bit. And here I am up in my chair and bright and cheerful today and ready to go so I might as well start. Do you want to hear the first one? Here, I'll read it out for you.

What is the thing you are not saying. No, I'm kidding. I can be a lot of fun at parties. Here it is, Name ten things you would like to say yes to. Oh, that's terrible. There's nothing to work with there. Shall we try another? The thing I am most worried about is . . . These questions have no life in them! None at all! Let's try another, I feel happiest when . . . Or, I couldn't live without . . .

No, I don't think there's anything to say. Maybe when the birds come back, maybe in the spring. Isn't April the month for *telling secrets? It's too cold now anyway, any words I say will freeze before they leave my mouth. And I was feeling so well and wonderful.*

Why does no one think to ask the important questions? I can't understand. What about, What does the smell of an orange remind you of? Or they could have tried, Who was the last person who touched you? Who was the last person you touched? Who taught you to cut a chain of snowflakes from a single sheet of paper? If you had a boxwood hedge would you carve it into straight lines or would you let it grow wild. Do you believe the last three things you were told. Do you think there's an art to opening locked doors. Do you believe in opening locked doors at all. Are we talking French doors or pocket doors or hinged doors or barn doors? What are the colours of the doors in your dreams. The doors you open and the doors that stay locked, how do you know the difference before you touch them. Ask me that, I could say, then maybe we could find something to talk about.

If we love someone enough they'll come back to us only better. We only have to believe things enough to make them true.

You're the only one who comes back you know. The universe is flying apart slowly and will never come back together, never ever again. The centres drop out of things all the time and we lose our favourite things and never find them. We're farther away today than we ever were before from everything else. But when you leave, I can say see you tomorrow. See you tomorrow. See? I can say see you tomorrow every day.

If I were to speak specifically though, if I were to let, say, the words fall like spiders out of my mouth, if I were to tell you something really terrible, would you come back? Would we still pretend to eat chocolates? Would you stand there next to me almost touching me, the way you do when you wipe out my little sink? Would you still? If I were to pull the terrible thing inch by inch, like a long blind eel, shrieking, out of my throat?

Everyone knows what they want me to say, everyone is waiting for me to say it. Don't think I don't know that. Don't think I don't understand that! Don't think I don't see it, them all standing around me with their bald featherless old vulture heads, waiting to dip their miserable beaks in underneath my ribs where I am raw and red and bloated.

What I'm trying to tell you is there's only screaming all the way down my throat, and the thing they're waiting for, it's only noise, it's only sound, it's all there and I'm already saying it and I'm always saying it and it's nothing, it's nothing but noise.

Part Three

15

The apartment was quiet after M left, but it wasn't an easy kind of quiet, more like the waiting and watching kind. The hitch that comes at the end of a long deep drawn-in breath. I wanted to go to the park. I wanted to spread out our picnic blanket and lie down on top of it and sleep until M was back and would be back in the apartment with us. I wanted to sleep until I wasn't alone, however long that took.

I wanted to have the days made into something that could be gotten rid of, like curtains that turned out after all to be the wrong kind of grey. All the weeks then, all the days, leaving in May, coming in June, and curling down and deeper as July and August slid heavily over the top of us, could be returned, discreetly, and with the proper excuse. Wrong shade, I could have written on a company form. Not as advertised.

We were moving now though through the deepest part of August, and of course there was no and never any turning back. The air was thick with rain and heavy and hot with storms. I was like a sailor being pulled under the water along the bottom of a big old ship, each day was scraping above me, all the hours, each one of them, were barnacles tearing open my back. I ran over to E's bed and shook her by the shoulder. Wake up, I said. Wake up! The day is coming whether we want it to or not! She opened her eyes and hugged me and I became real for a moment. We went to the park.

I packed up B and E and we jumped through the back window. We sat by the pump and I unpacked the little boxes with things inside to eat. Cucumbers and grapes. Crackers with seeds and crackers with no seeds. We sat for a long time before anyone else came but eventually Nell arrived and I realized then that I'd been waiting for her. She set her blanket down very close to mine even though the park was empty and there was plenty of space.

She unwound her wrap and plucked out the baby and set him down on the blanket, kicked off her shoes and lay down next to him, the baby, and next to me too in a way. Then she propped herself up a bit and turned to me and said what could have been almost anything. Her turning to me, talking, after all the afternoons I'd been watching her, well, it was exhilarating. A bit like jumping into a cold lake. You can't imagine it before it happens, the feeling. But there was no reply that I could make of course. I caught, I thought, the word for children and so I smiled a bit when she stopped talking. Her eyes told me she'd said something funny. She frowned and tried again and then I had to say, I'm sorry I don't speak French. The words spilled all over the place like groceries from a ripped bag, and that was it I realized. That was as far as I could get. I was like a swimmer turning back to shore. I couldn't go any further towards her. What had I been expecting to happen?

I called E back and packed us up and left. We had to get to the market anyway, we had to. I was going to cook a real dinner tonight and we would eat oranges for dessert that would be so sweet that we would remember them for ever. We would find oranges at the market that could not be gotten anywhere else.

I bought tomatoes and a bag of oranges. I bought two bottles of wine. Local stuff. Chasselas. E picked a bag of chocolates wrapped in the colours of the Swiss flag, and I thought why not? And I smiled at her and bought them. Why not why not why not. The shopping bags were heavy and the little plastic handles cut into my hands. I didn't have the stroller so I carried B too and walked slowly down the street like an apple tree with everything just hanging off me. E laughed and skipped ahead and I made my face ready to smile, just in case she looked back at me but she didn't, so I let my mouth sag because sometimes it just is what it is.

A tram pulled up and the doors opened and E ran ahead into the crowd screaming and laughing like I had done at the beach as a child chasing gulls. Well what difference was there anyway. We made it home and I hoisted us up through the window and I put away our food in all the places that I had determined were the right ones. Tomatoes on the counter and so on.

The apartment was dark though it was barely afternoon. I wheeled the shutters down on the back window anyway. The metal slats shrieked a little as they slipped into place and I thought I should really tell the rental company about this because soon the whole thing might rust up tight and trap us. I was thinking this, thinking, I should call them right now and tell them, when I saw something in the darkness, something that crept up behind the closing shutters, something like a face but also not, something with eyes made out of dust maybe, eyes that were so familiar and so strange. I blinked though and it was gone and I thought, something is wrong, but also I thought there's no time for anything to be wrong, for anything not to be fine and exactly right.

Later, I put E to bed early, tucked her in tight. I pulled the sheet down on top of her and pushed it under the mattress inch by inch. She fell asleep while I did this, while I told her goodnight goodnight sweet dreams.

When E was little, I mean when she was a baby, before B was born, M was very good at singing her lullabies when she couldn't sleep at night. Many nights, when she cried out, he went to her instead of me and picked her up and walked her gently in circles around and around and around her room. I would listen to them, her maybe crying a little, maybe beginning to calm down, him singing quietly. Just a handful of songs but over and over and over again. Promising her, I suppose, that everything was beautiful and nothing would ever end. It would have been easy to listen to that song I mean and think it was a promise like that.

I've never been a singer though, my voice, it always comes out in pieces. Scratchy. Not soothing, not what she needed, E I mean, when she cried. So, when I went to get her, I would whisper to her. I was too tired to think of much to say. Sometimes I told her that I was so tired that it felt like my bed was a foreign country. A homeland I could no longer properly imagine. The beds in our house, sometimes, I would whisper too, look like they will look after the apocalypse. Empty. Waiting for people who can never come back to them. Mostly though, I kept it simple. I would cut to the chase. I would whisper, We are the only people in the world.

We are the only people in the world, I would say to her. The only ones. The only ones the only ones

*   *   *

It was time next for B to go to bed, but he wasn't ready. He couldn't be put down. So I turned off all the lights in the apartment and walked with him in a little circle that took in all the rooms. Round and round the garden. Like two teddy bears. One step. Two step. Tickle you under there. Do you know that one? I said to him.

We whispered goodnight to all the things as we saw them. Over and over again we did. Snips and snails and puppy dog tails.

Goodnight kitchen, goodnight floor,
goodnight windows, goodnight door.
Goodnight rags and sprays and mops,
goodnight shutters, goodnight locks.

In my downy lullaby voice, I could say anything at all. His hair was so soft against my face. I could feel him and smell him in the dark so completely. There wasn't a word for it really, what there was between him and me, it was something different, something total, something only for us.

There were things that I didn't say goodnight to. Things that I refused to talk to him about, lullaby voice or no. I didn't mention the whispering inside the walls. The slurp gurgle of the drains. The shadows that grew longer and longer, longer, really, than the flickering lights should have let them.

Finally B fell asleep, sagging all at once against me in the most horrible/wonderful, horridful, way and I set him down in his crib. This was what it was to be a good mother. My fingernails were dirty and too long but who was there to see me? So I reached down into his crib and brushed the hair off his forehead with my scab-crusted hands. I blew him kisses, one two three, for good luck and goodnight. Sweet dreams. See you in the morning. Shhhh.

I waited then, after I was done laying him down, for whatever had been gathering to come and get me, but the apartment was quiet and empty and the dust stayed only dust. I bagged up the trash in the kitchen, the bits of dinner that couldn't be saved for another day, the peels and the rinds and the egg shells. I cinched it all up tight and put it in the guest room, against the wall on the far side of the room, away from the shopping bags, away from the eiderdown.

I dripped a little water onto the plant and turned it a quarter turn. It was looking sick, its tentacles were turning a pale water-logged green as if they were drowning from the inside out. Perhaps I was doing everything wrong for it. I turned it another quarter turn and left. Well what else could I have done? It's impossible, isn't it? Always having to decide what will be saved.

Once I wiped down the counters there would be nothing else to do until morning. I could sit or stand or float or run around and around and around the rooms as long as I was quiet. For a while I scritch scratched the knives against the sharpening stone. The angle is so important, the exact angle of the blade against the stone. Three strokes on one side of the blade, three strokes on the other, one hand on the handle, the pads of index and middle fingers balanced at the tip. Scritching and scratching. Precision, concentration. Afterwards, test it.

Feel how, with a sharp blade, a thing can be cut without resistance. Without any resistance at all.

There was a smell in the apartment, something nice, warm wax and wicks burning and when I left the kitchen to investigate I found the table all lit up with candles as if for a dinner party. In between the candles the table was strewn with matches of all sizes like confetti and something sunk in me then, all cold like a heavy thing going fast through water. Something that just plunged right through me I mean, and I thought that I could see someone sitting at the far end of the table in a chair pulled out just for her. But of course it was all only smoke.

At some point I slept because I woke on the floor in the bedroom. The room was already hot and I was sweating because, I found, I was wearing my long brown coat all buttoned up from top to bottom. E came into the room, sleepy, and asked me about it, about the coat, why I was wearing it over my pyjamas and I said, thinking quickly, Well I thought today we'd stay in the apartment and play explorers. How does that sound? We can play all day together right here, I told her. Doesn't that sound like great big buckets of fun?

The bruises on my face and arm were almost gone now but in the half-light of the apartment they could look on my skin like the leafy shadows of equatorial trees. We could pretend like the dusty socks that were accumulating on the floor were the eyes of crocodiles floating in a muddy river.

We could pretend that the beds were flat-bottomed river boats gliding over all the things we couldn't see. We wouldn't have to leave the apartment. I wasn't even really sure if I could get my hands to open the door.

I bolted both locks and did up the security chain. Feeling suddenly like there were eyes watching me, I covered over the peephole with tape. I put tape too over the face of the clock in the kitchen because we were alone alone alone and we could eat when we were hungry and sleep when we were tired and be as free as birds inside here where we already were. Where we would stay.

I made lemonade and spilled the sugar on the counter, all the little crystals tinkling like sand made out of glass or bones. There! I said triumphantly. Now the ants will come! But I felt, well a breath, or something like a breath, shiver down the back of my neck and I remembered those eyes made out of dust or something else and I cleaned up all the sugar and bit my knuckles quick for luck.

I cut the last cucumber into shapes that were supposed to look like monkeys or tropical flowers. E could barely pick them up, they were that thin and slippery. We ended up licking them off the table like wild animals. Sometimes my heart would begin to beat hard and I would gasp to catch my breath but mostly it was lovely. A whole day spent picnicking in the shade.

It could have been late or it could have been early whenever we went to bed. I took E and B with me. We all piled in together.

E and B drifted off smiling and I lay there with them, loving them that much. It was like that sometimes, being a mother, like feeling all the screws tighten down inside you.

Eventually I untwined myself from E and took B to his crib. I wanted to take the garbage out but that sticky shutter wouldn't let me so I just scooped all the leftover food into another black plastic bag and even a plate or two that I couldn't see my way through to cleaning and set it down in the guest room next to the other bags of garbage. The flies smiled then and rubbed their little hands together like good children. I came back into the kitchen and arranged the alphabet letters on the fridge to say I love you for E to see even though she couldn't read yet.

The point was now mainly to move quickly. The point was to be quicker than whatever was coming, slipping into the apartment like bad thoughts, to be busy enough that whatever it was that was there couldn't get me. The darkness, the child, the dusty eyes. To be quicker and necessary and needed and full of love. To move and move and move through all the hours until the children woke and were ready to play and keep me high and dry and safe from winking out inside my clothes and disappearing into nothing. What is a mother anyway when her children are asleep? What could she possibly be? If a tree falls in the forest. It's like that isn't it?

I found more candles burning, this time in the bathroom, lighting up my face in the mirror, the little flames merry and just so almost touching the bottom of the towel. It would have been almost cheerful, like dinner parties in the bathtub, except it wasn't and though I blew them out quick, the candles, I knew that it was too late and that the thing was inside with me anyway already. The shadow, the toad, whatever it was, hopped and crouched and sniffed at this at that. It was moving through the rooms looking for me. I could feel it, could see it slipping in and out of the corners of my eyes. I had used too much bleach in the cleaning water and my hands were speckled with raw patches on them and stung like anything but I couldn't stop dipping my hands into the cleaning bucket and wiping down the kitchen counter because otherwise it would surely find me. I told myself, licking the sweat off the top of my lip, to lie down, still in the tall grass. The thing, the terrible thing, it hadn't happened yet. I was still, thank god and goodness, in the time before.

Something banged against the shutters in the bedroom. It came again. Bang. It could have been a bottle or a ball or a fist pounding the metal slats. Bang. Bang. Bang. The noise woke E and she sat up and cried out for me and I couldn't move until I was sure the thing in the apartment was gone and I was alone again and safe. I dumped the bucket of bleach and water down the sink and rinsed out the little towel and wrapped my hands, because they were bleeding now from the bleach and all the washing, in more towels so they wouldn't stain the rental-company sheets and then I ran to E and kissed her and tucked myself in with her and slept and slept.

16

When I woke, the bed was washed in weak shuttered-up sunlight. My hands had escaped from the towels and found their way into E's hair. There wasn't much of a mess because the raw spots from the bleach had scabbed over which was a relief considering the sheets.

It was morning or afternoon, daytime anyway. M could have been anywhere and we were here. I threw myself at the window and managed to get the shutters up and the window open but it was hard going and I almost couldn't do it. Opening it left me sweating and dizzy and I leaned back against the window frame and really knew, in that moment, that it was time to run. The window was open beside me. It was right there. But how could I have done a thing like that?

There were yellow shoes under the window, lying in the grass. They were perfectly arranged and waiting, calm yellow shoes, as if the person wearing them had, woosh, been lifted up out of them and carted off. The grass around the shoes was trampled down in all directions.

E woke up and was hungry and there was no avoiding going to the store today. We needed yogurt, milk, berries. I grabbed my coat and E and jumped out of the window. B was still asleep and I thought if I just do this one thing quickly, if I just leave him here and run, I'll be able to get him a warm roll and won't even have to wake him. He can't, I thought, he almost certainly can't, get out of his crib on his own. Hurrying, I slipped my feet into the little yellow shoes, they were at least two sizes too small for me but I squeezed into them anyway and, carrying E, ran off to the store. See? I said shouting as we ran a bit through the wet grass and hopped over the planter out onto the sidewalk, See? Isn't this fun? We'll be back before B wakes up. He'll think we flew.

At the store I filled my bag with this and that, grabbing anything. As the minutes passed I felt less sure about leaving B, less sure that he wouldn't wake, less sure that he couldn't get out of his crib. The seconds twisted into me and I felt the whole world tightening around my shoulders. I fought for berries with all the other greasy-haired mothers, we all needed the best. We all, each one of us specifically, needed the best berries with which to feed our very special children. We all took turns fingering the avocados. We looked at each other out of the corners of our eyes. We peered down into each other's shopping baskets. They were too ripe, the avocados. Slightly too. We recoiled. We all knew about vitamins and nutrients, we all knew about the dangers of over-ripe and under-ripe fruit. We all knew all about it.

The girl ringing up the purchases beeped through everyone's baskets very slowly. Everyone in line in front of me had baskets filled with things. When it was finally my turn I slammed the croissants down so hard that half of them were flattened, and the checkout girl, young, solicitous, with no baby at home, either inside his crib and smothering or outside and imperilled by literally every single thing, sent the shop assistant all the way to the back of the store to get new uncrushed and freshly baked ones.

Outside, E wanted to walk. She was tired of being carried. I put her down and tried to make a game out of running together. See? I couldn't see the apartment. It was just around the corner but I couldn't see it. I began to find breathing difficult and a pain started up in my chest.

E, I said, E, let's run. But she wouldn't. She walked slower and slower until she wasn't moving at all just standing there looking at me. The handles of the shopping bags cut into my bleach-cracked hands and suddenly, in a moment, in the blink of an eye, all the strength ran out of my legs. It was like falling down a waterfall. I was drowning right there on the street with my groceries.

I slid down onto the sidewalk and then, because I really couldn't see the apartment, because leaving B had been a mistake, because leaving at all had been, I began to crawl along on the pavement on my stomach, dragging the bags, dragging my useless legs. It's a game, see? I shouted now to E. It's a game! Even as I shouted I felt the dried noodles, the tubs of yogurt pressing into my shoulders, pegging me, as brutally as a dog's teeth, to the ground. From the apartment, I heard B begin to cry.

Skipping, crawling, dragging, jumping, we made it back to the window with almost all of our things. I tossed the groceries through the open window, then I tossed E after them. I kicked the shoes back into the grass and threw myself over the window sill as well. Threshold. Maison magique. Husk. Hull. Cocoon. Hide as in skin. Hide as in to.

I lowered the shrieking shutters back down and it was half dark again and safe, except of course the eyes that suggested themselves in the swirling dust. B had fallen out of his crib and was lying on his back beside it kicking his legs and putting his hands one after the other into his mouth. His cheeks were covered in little red marks, a swarm of tiny bites or kisses.

I cooed over him and kissed him and checked his pupils to make sure they were the same size. He'd fallen on a pile of blankets. I promised him, whispering and singing and cuddling and swinging him around and around until he laughed, that I wouldn't leave again. That we would all stay and stay and stay inside where we were safe and cosy and together.

E had a bloody knee. I hadn't seen her fall on the way back but she must have and I whisked her off to the bathroom and drew a bath for her and sat her in the warm soapy water and even dangled my legs in the bath beside her and smiled and didn't take my eyes off her so she would know that I was with her and loved her always. We let the water get higher and higher and higher. We let it slop over the edges. We laughed when it did because we loved each other so much.

When the water started to get cold I plucked her out of it and wrapped her in three different towels and set her on the bed like a baby. She loved this game and I told her over and over how little she was and kissed her and wrapped her tighter and tighter until she couldn't move. Then I dried her hair and brushed it and braided it and she dressed herself and I actually started humming as I tidied up.

There was a smell in the bathroom. That grey rotting-meat smell that comes from drains. I sprayed the tub with disinfectant. The cuts on my hands were singing with all the wet but still, the smell didn't go away so I jumped into the tub and stuck my hand all the way down inside the drain as far as it would go. I twisted my fingers down around inside it.

There were rotten gobs of hair mixed up with all sorts of other filth. I pulled these out bit by bit and set them in a line beside the drain like a tiny horde of stinking mice. When I'd pulled out all I could I dumped some bleach down the drain to take care of the rest. The micey filth balls I grabbed up in my hands and held them slimy-dripping for one long second before I dumped them all into the trash. I washed and washed my hands and even though it was filthy to do one thing and then another, I ran into the kitchen to make something for

E to eat because she would need it and I was the only one there to get it for her.

When I was little, I saw my mother once, crouching naked and wet in the shower in our musty blue apartment bathroom. She had her back to me and her long wet hair streamed down across the secret map of her skin. She was picking long wet clumps of our hair out of the drain. She didn't turn when I opened the door, she just got on with it. She might have been crying or it could have been the water from the shower on her face.

When she finished, she grabbed them all up, the grey flecked nests of dead hair, and flushed them down the toilet. Then she walked over to me, reached up above me and shut the door and didn't come out for the rest of the morning. I had to pee in the bushes behind the parking lot.

Afterwards, I never wanted to be left alone in any place. It was something about the hair, how much of it there was. If we were always losing so much of ourselves, how could we be sure of what we'd have left, what would stick?

Also, naturally, I always had a horror of drains, it seemed to me the loneliest, the most unloved thing a woman could do, crouching naked over a pipe, fishing out wretched bits of her own hair.

I made E spaghetti with butter for lunch and cucumbers and carrots all cut up into the tiniest pieces. The cups in the kitchen were filled with ash, they kept filling up with the stuff and I kept dumping it all down the drain. Hot ash and cold ash. Ashes on fingers, ashes on our toes, ashes lining the tops of our lips like milk moustaches. Ring around the rosey, pocket full of posey . . . It was from the candles though, that I found sometimes burning in the kitchen or the cabinets.

We pretended the carrots were butterflies and we were frogs with long tongues. She slurped the pasta up, hunting the butterflies with her wide frog's mouth.

That afternoon we played more games. I'll be the mother bear and you can be the baby, I said. We'll spend all winter in our cave eating berries. Outside it's snowing, it's all ice and cold and terrible things. Come here little bear, I said, and I'll lick your fur and scratch your fuzzy ears. Come here little bear, I said, we'll be so warm together in our cave.

We scratched up the paint on the walls with our bear claws. The walls had been painted over so many times in cheap rubbery paint that the layers came off in great big sheets, exactly like tree bark. This is the real thing! I said in my growly honeycomb voice. I told E, This is what bears do to sharpen their claws. If we were bears, our claws would be so sharp now, we could slice right through the door.

We made toast and E and I buttered it with big melting swipes and set hunks of cheese on top. We crunched it up sitting on the rental-company sofa and we didn't care at all about the crumbs. We rolled around on top of them and let them fall through all the cracks between the cushions. I unstuffed the couch pillows looking for something, I can't remember what, keys maybe, but we made that a game too, so it would be fun. Foam and plastic rental-company feathers flying up everywhere in the air and then down around us as we cuddled on the sofa. Has someone been pinching your arm? I asked E, looking at it. Red marks crept all over her smooth skin. She didn't answer.

I sat on the sofa and nursed B until he fell asleep. Perhaps we all slept. Who knows? It could have been the middle of the night.

When I woke up it was dark outside. B was still on top of me sleeping in his soft full-bellied baby way. I slid him carefully down into his crib and went to go find E. E, I said. E, in my soft voice. She didn't answer. E, I said, where are you? Where are you where are you? I was creeping along the hallway towards the bedrooms bent over almost double like an old witch limping through the forest with her basket of apples. Or maybe I was loping like a wolf. It was the middle of the night, so anything was possible.

E, I said, E, it's me. Where are you? It was so dark in the hall. I couldn't see a thing and the dry dry cracked backs of my hands rustled against the walls like dead leaves. There was a light on in her bedroom, and a soft humming coming like singing from her room. Good evening, the hush-soft humming could have said. Good night, with roses covered.

E, I said, but my voice was too quiet for anyone to have heard me, it was as if the apartment itself was gulping down my words, was drinking up any sound that I could make. Perhaps I could have screamed right then and no one would have heard me. There was a noise at the front door, the hushed slip of a long coat gliding. Had I locked the door? Had I remembered to? It wasn't M outside in the hall, coming back from wherever he had been, it wasn't him. It didn't feel like him. There was a scraping against the door that could have been a knock, could have been knuckles on wood.

I was in the entryway now. M? I said. M? Is that you? The doorknob rattled and I felt how cold it was suddenly in the apartment, too cold for the summer when the nights should have been long and cheerful and we should never be alone. The whispering started now from the other side of the door and I thought, Yes, now, I should open it. M? I said, but I couldn't reach out, couldn't lift my fingers to the lock. The light switched off in E's room. Click. I heard it and now the dark itself was cold and I ran back down the hall to E's room and I felt the thing skipping behind me. I felt the lightness of it, how quickly it could move. I threw open the door and threw myself onto her little bed and under the covers and found her there, warm and fast asleep. B was all alone out there, the beds were lifeboats maybe, in a cold ocean, and I couldn't be in two places at once. I shook her a little, but she was asleep and kept sleeping, asleep in a way that made her gone, that had taken her somewhere else. E, I whispered, but she wouldn't wake.

There was a soft clicking in the apartment, like the light in the kitchen being flicked on and off and on again. I had my head under the blanket and couldn't see. Perhaps it was playing with me. Perhaps this was all a sort of game. Click.

Click. The light in the hall flicked on, flicked off. I wasn't cold anymore but sweating under the blanket. I couldn't drop my hands down from my eyes. The light in the bedroom flicked on. Click. I found I couldn't scream, could only open my mouth with the scream stuck inside it. Bang. Something hit the shutters on the little window in E's room. Bang bang bang. The light clicked off.

I threw off the blanket and started banging on the window myself, from the inside. E's body bounced lightly on the mattress but she didn't wake. Still, she was elsewhere. Then the thing was behind me in the room, bang bang bang, I shoved my fingers into the metal slats and tried to lift them up but the window was shut tight. We were stuck. Help, I screamed, Help help help, but no one could hear my voice, the apartment rushed in to eat it up and I could hear how quiet we were despite my desperate noise.

Soft behind me, like a dancing partner, something came and slid a cold hand up my arm and touched my bruises, and another hand went gently like a couple dancing slowly in the moonlight and like hush-now-it's-all-fine around my neck.

B screamed, loud and wailing, in his normal hungry-baby voice and I was alone again in the apartment with nothing there.

I ran fast to him like any good mother in the middle of the night and picked him up and cuddled him and lifted up my shirt and slipped my nipple into his mouth and he sucked a little and fell back asleep and didn't seem bothered that I was shaking and soaked in sweat. He had more red marks on his cheeks, a rash of little kisses. I set him down in his crib and whispered I love you and sweet dreams and all the things that good mothers say over the soft heads of their sleeping children. Then I crawled into the guest room and over to the garbage side of the floor. I didn't want to stain the beautiful white sheets, the eiderdown, all still in their bags and waiting for a bed. The bed that would make the whole room fantastic. Beautiful and perfect, whites and blues, a whole island stocked with little jewelled soaps and smelling of sea salt and cotton.

The garbage was starting to smell but I didn't mind it now. I liked it maybe and the mould from the lemons in the bowl puffed up into the air like green smoke if I touched them, just giving themselves up like that into nothing and I liked that too. Who is touching me, I didn't think, didn't ask the lemons, didn't show them my arms, my face, my neck.

I thought, I should call M. I should tell him to come home, but I only thought it quietly. Besides, I had found it floating, my phone I mean, in the mop bucket, all soaked through and abandoned, its face gone blank and dead in the grey water. Now, I took the phone out of my pocket and set it in the crack between the guest-room door and the wall and crushed it slowly, using the door, just watching the screen bend, then feeling it give, feeling it break richly under the weight of my hands.

I curled up behind the bags as if they were some kind of fortress and closed my eyes. Click. Maybe I heard the lights in the apartment. Maybe there was someone at the door, but I was safe in the guest room behind the garbage. Maybe I was. I covered my eyes and lay still in my burrow as the hours passed and listened for the sounds of my children, ready to jump straight up if they needed me. I'm here, I'm here, I would shout if they asked for me. Don't worry, I'll always be right here with you.

17

The days folded together like a map crumpling in on itself, continents crashed, tectonic plates ground together like bad teeth, oceans dropped away to nothing. I made food for E, bits and pieces of things that got wilder as our cupboards were stripped down to their studs. We licked the food off our plates and stopped using forks and knives. Dried pasta we could crunch in our teeth. We painted our arms with the last of the bottled sauces and whooped at each other.

E began to look a bit pale, dark circles flowered beneath her eyes. I told her she was a garden inside a garden inside a garden and hugged her tight and close. She began keeping her animals in a box under her bed. She didn't want me to play with them even though I offered. Let's get out baby giraffe, I would say, let's get him out and let him run around the tops of the curtains. He's asleep, she said. Don't wake him up. The others? Baby orangutan? They're all asleep, she said. Every morning she woke up with more red marks.

XOXO is for hugs and kisses. Bites mean I love you so much I'll eat you up. There was an old owl who lived in an oak, whiskey, whaskey, weedle, I told her. And all the words he ever spoke were fiddle, faddle, feedle.

There was someone else, I was sure, in the apartment, making E's bed, tending to her. When I went to check on her in the middle of the night her sheets were always tucked up perfectly tight, right underneath her chin. One morning I found all her clothes folded and put away, the corners of all her little shirts teased into sharp angles, looking like they'd all been pressed with an iron. Sometimes I thought I heard someone singing to B while he slept, sometimes I sort of startled awake and found it was me that was doing it, me that was singing.

At night, when the children were asleep, I thought about Nell. The banging on the window didn't come again but I wondered, had it been her out there? Running away from something? Had she seen us jumping out of that window? Had she been looking for a window to jump into? Had she had her children with her? The baby? The boy? Had she left her shoes as a sign? Or had she been lifted up out of them? I could think about these things at night, in the dark, when I was waiting for the children to need me, biting at my nails and my fingers. Something about it just let my mind run and run but in the end all I could think about were the dusty eyes in the dark that came out when I closed the shutters, and how they, the eyes, looked so much like my own. What I'm trying to say is that sometimes there isn't anywhere to skip to, only long hours that stretch like oil, glistening and sliding over the tops of all the stretching shadows.

There were so many flies now in the apartment that we all took to wearing long sleeves so we couldn't feel their legs on our skin. B was sleeping so much. He was like a bear in winter I suppose. Such a good baby, sleeping and sleeping and sleeping in my arms. He was so light I almost never had to put him down, and we could dance for hours like two feathers, floating up and up, impervious to gravity and time.

We hid under the ruined sofa cushions. I stuffed my clothes with the feathers and the foam and made a scarecrow person. I made one too for E and a tiny little lumpy one for B. So that we could each have a scarecrow version of ourselves to sit next to and talk to. What's three plus three? I asked E, pointing at the scarecrow family and then pointing at ourselves. What's two plus four? I asked, sitting E down among the scarecrow people. See? Do you see how it stays the same no matter where you go?

There were so many things to do. Once E woke up with her hair braided into two gorgeous plaits, one on each side of her head. The braids glinted in her half-dark room like oil lamps, and we admired her hair in the bathroom together. How beautiful we are, I whispered to her. Look at us. But I wondered a bit, if I let myself, who had done the braiding.

I imagined rust growing on the outside of the metal shutters. We played with the light switches, flicking them fast on and off and on and off until they began burning out one by one. We loved the way they snapped and fizzed, the lights, when they burned out, the way the light flickered and grew huge and hectic just before it was gone. In the end we were left with only the candles and we set these up around the apartment, at the table, we ate at all hours by their light.

We pretended we lived in the woods. Or sometimes that we had gone to sleep and wouldn't wake again for a hundred years. E wrote messages for me in the alphabet letters on the fridge and I would spend a long time at night trying to decode their mysteries, constellations of vowels and consonants that were so carefully arranged. Help me, I said to the letters. Really. Now. Really help me now. But of course I could never read them right and she was so many years away from learning how to spell.

E took to following me around the apartment, whispering, knock knock. The beginning of a joke. Only the first part though, she never said the rest. The game went on and on until I felt like a wound, gaping, food for invisible things. Knock knock, she said, over and over, as if there was no part of me that wouldn't open if she asked. Maybe she just wanted to get outside. The games I played had to get better, brighter, much much much more fun. They had to keep us all happy, they had to keep us all inside. We painted the walls with a mixture of honey and flour and the last bit of glue E had from a bottle in her craft supplies bag. We painted this too on the walls in the bathroom and watched the flies get stuck.

But, more and more, E wasn't asking about games and B was so sleepy he was barely even ever awake. Perhaps I should have called a doctor, or run out of the house down the street. We could still play though, so in a way, we were fine. B was quiet and we were quiet and quiet was good.

It was really night outside, that really dark kind of night that you can feel even with your eyes closed, even with the shutters on your windows shut tight. The kind of middle-of-the-night dark that touches your skin with its fingers all over and makes you shiver. That kind of dark. I'd tried to keep E awake as long as I could. Stay awake honey, stay awake baby, just one more game with Mommy, look we'll be like this or this. We'll be fawns and have a tea party under a tree, look at our hooves, our jam pies! Our hot mugs of tea! But she had said she was tired, that she felt sick, that she was hungry and couldn't eat any more cold rice with syrup even though I told her a million times how delicious that kind of dinner was, how lucky she was to have it, how it could have been anything we imagined it to be.

Anyway she took her animals and went to bed, closed the door to her little room and shut me out. I thought about scratching at her door and saying I was a baby goat, asking her if I could crawl into bed with her for just a moment but I didn't. It was really good and healthy if she wanted to be alone. It was amazing that she wasn't afraid of the dark. More afraid of me I thought and had to break the thought with a quick hard laugh to make it not be true. How could she be afraid of me? We loved each other so much. I loved her with a feeling that sometimes crushed my own lungs and made me not able to breathe.

I hovered at the edge of B's crib to see if he would wake up and need me. B? I whispered so quietly. B? I whispered a bit louder but he was asleep and fine all by himself and so I was alone and then I wasn't and then I was really afraid.

Right now, I thought, right now I am afraid. I'm not laughing. I'm not imagining that I'm afraid. I really am, right now, here, crouching between the crib and the rental-company sofa. Click. The light in the kitchen, the last one, clicked off and the apartment was dark like the inside of a mouth. Click. It came back on again but brighter than it had been. I shut my eyes. Dishes clinked in the kitchen like a breeze was running through the cupboards. I pressed my hands to the side of my face covering my ears. Maybe if I was still enough this would go away. I wanted to wake B. B! I would have screamed. E! But my mouth was shut down tight and I couldn't make any sounds come out.

There were footsteps running in the kitchen, plates being set on the table, and cups and glasses as if I were listening to my own ghost setting out breakfast. As if I were dead and still trying to get the kids ready to go to the park, slicing cold cucumbers with my so-sharp knives. You can hear me. Said the voice that I couldn't hear. Said the voice in a voice that I knew. Come out come out wherever you are. I felt myself going white with cold that wasn't really cold. A cold that was deeper than cold, that started from inside me, from inside my bones. I was trembling. Soon I would start to shake so much that I would give myself away. I would lose myself to that feeling pulling now right over me, that feeling of being about to be found. If you go down to the woods today, the voice said, you're sure of a big surprise. And I whispered back in my shaking voice, because of course I couldn't help it, If you go down to the woods today you'd better go in disguise. And there was a delighted laugh that came from close by and the sound of two hands clapping quick together.

The terrible thing, I thought. The terrible thing.

The light clicked on in the little hall between the kitchen and the living room. The light so bright in the shell of the burned-out bulb that it was as if my eyes weren't squeezed shut tight. As if I were thrown suddenly into the sun. I could smell the electricity. The burning. The lights clicked off. Nimble running steps, pattering like rain on the carpet, so soft and dancing. Slipping one way, then another. The light clicked on again. The light clicked off.

B snored a bit and moved his arm. Fell deeper and deeper into the deep cold ocean of sleep and dreams and being away when people need you. Help me.

For years, when I was little, when I wasn't little anymore, I felt my way to the bathroom at night, refusing to open my eyes in the dark. As long as I kept my eyes closed I was safe. I would have one more second before I knew, and this was worth all the bruises on my shins, even once a broken toe. This was worth it, the not knowing. The refusing to.

Any second the light would click on in the living room and there I would be and not asleep. If only I had been asleep I would have been safe, of this I was certain, but I wasn't. Perhaps I would have to act first. Jump up, scream, make a noise loud enough to surprise it. Roar at it maybe, roar it away from me fast and now.

Click. The light came on. I leapt up from behind the crib screaming, my chest heaving, the breath not behaving in my throat, and there I was. Another me, smiling. What I'm trying to tell you is that I was right there in front of me, wearing my long brown coat. My hair was done up nicely. I even had a little make up on. I was standing there smiling in the smoking burning light. What I'm trying to tell you is that the red lips framing her teeth were mine. I grabbed the baby, thank God I did. Thank God I thought to grab him. He didn't wake, he was hot and limp against my shoulder. The me across the room frowned a little and then I ran and the me that didn't have the baby took one second to realize that I was running and I used that second to throw open the door to E's room and grab her too out of the dark and then I was running for the door and I would never make it and who was to say anyway that making it to the door would mean we would be safe. Who was there really that could say that?

There was a burning smell that became stronger as I ran down the hallway, and the heat in the apartment suddenly rose like hands against my face, pushing me back. I wrapped us all in my arms and ran down the hallway, with me, the other me, I knew, coming after. We were both just as fast as each other.

Stop, I heard her say, in my voice exactly. Stop. What are you doing? And there was fear in her voice, which of course was mine, a wild fear that I hadn't expected. Give them back to me, she said. Then there was smoke and real flames and my hand grabbed the door handle and it was so hot that my skin smoked and stuck to it. The apartment was on fire. There was real fire all around us, eating everything up. The apartment was on fire and all the locks were done up tight.

I ripped at the bolts, at the smoking chain, I felt the skin of my hand give way under the heat and then I didn't feel it. I grabbed the handle and pushed and we fell through the door and out of the apartment and out and out and out into the hallway outside. I slammed the door behind us savagely, and I heard her scream. I mean I heard her scream my scream, scream the way that I would have, long and with exactly my voice. She screamed the names of the children, of course she did. I would have.

A woman came running towards us down the hallway with a scratchy woollen blanket. She tried to take E and B from me but I wouldn't let her, my arms were locked that hard around them, so instead she held the blanket around us all together and walked us outside and to an ambulance waiting in the car park, saying things I couldn't understand in a soothing voice. We were safe she could have been saying, we were the ones that were safe.

18

E and B and I were tucked into the back of an ambulance and driven away. At the hospital, nurses peeled E and B off me gently. I was told that B was dehydrated, that he was sick, was perhaps quite ill, but would recover. That they had both inhaled a lot of smoke. My hand was the only thing keeping me there, nailing me into the room I mean. The pain in my hand was a white line so bright it stopped my thoughts. The nurses wrapped it in cling film and then in gauze. It was better not to look at it.

After my hand was taken care of, to the extent that it could be, I found B and E in beds next to each other, each fitted with little plastic masks that were held tight against their mouths with soft elastic bands. Miles and miles of plastic tubes wrapped around them like fishing lines that would pull them back to shore, to me, into my arms.

They looked so dirty in the clean hospital sheets. Their faces were smudged and crusted with old dinners and who knew what else. E's hair was tangled, it looked exactly like a cloud of flies swarming around her face. What must we look like out here, I thought, and I wished for just one second that we were back inside the apartment where no one could see us. The red marks it turned out were only lipstick, were and had been only kisses after all. The nurses wiped them all away, all the kisses all the red layers of them, coaxing the new clean skin out into the bright hospital lights.

I was given a chair to sit on and this I positioned exactly equidistant between the two beds. I promised myself that I would leap up at any moment where leaping was necessary. B was asleep but it was a better kind of sleep now, a safe-at-last kind of sleep and not the kind of sleep he had been sleeping before. I put my bandaged hand near him on the bed and felt better. E looked severely at me as she almost always did, but took my other hand and held it as she drifted off too amid the beeps and bright lights. In her other hand she clutched her giraffe, another lone survivor. We were here, here we were.

A nurse brought me a thermos of tea and I drank it while she set up a cot against the opposite wall. She had blonde hair and a round sort of body a bit like a wheelbarrow, sort of blunt and tottering but perfect anyway for getting from place to place. I felt myself moved onto the cot. Perhaps she just scooped me up. Maybe she said something to me just then, maybe she told me I was a good mother. Maybe she told me I could rest now, that the machines would keep a better watch over B, over E anyway, that I could sleep and sleep and sleep and only wake up when I chose to. Maybe she was just asking for my insurance card.

In the morning we woke up and were cared for, a thermos of fennel tea for me, apricot juice for E, thick and as orange as a duck's foot. A nurse came in to wash B, plunking him in and out of a small portable tub filled with soapy water while I watched and held his hand. I showered and washed myself as best I could with the tiny hospital soap. Afterwards I was exhausted and slept again. E played all the time with her giraffe.

Mostly we waited for the hours to pass, but in an easy way. I nursed B off and on almost all day, at the encouragement of many friendly nurses. We were doing everything right, they might have been saying. We would all love each other for ever and could stay as long as we liked. E and I ate steak for dinner and for me a nurse brought a tiny glass of wine. At night we slept. For days we lived like babies, the three of us, eating, sleeping, being taken care of by inexplicable giants, until M came and found us.

There you are, he said when he walked into the room, smelling like ocean water, like he had just stepped off a plane from a sunny place and maybe he had.

He picked up E and hugged her and she let him hug her giraffe too. He picked up B then and hugged him and then he came and put his arms around me even though he still had E and B and her giraffe in his arms. Jesus, he said into my shoulder, you sure know how to scare a guy.

He let us go and wiped his eyes.

I got here as soon as I could, he said. I came as soon as I heard. You should see it, he said, the apartment building. The whole thing's gutted, completely burned.

How did it happen? I asked without knowing really what I was asking.

Police think it started in our corner of the building, M said. They say it might have been some woman, M said. They found her by the bins acting strangely I guess. They're still investigating.

An old woman? I asked.

Maybe, he said. He didn't know.

In a purple coat? I asked and he said again he didn't know. Then he looked at me in a way I didn't really want to be looked at, questioning something, so I didn't ask anything else. I thought though, about the old woman by the bins, about her licking her lips with her fingers in the garbage bags, her neat hair, her damp breath, her smell that hovered between shortbread, wet wool and rotten teeth. I thought about her counting out those coins on the table beside her empty coffee cup. Later I would say to the police that yes, I had seen a woman, once, by the bins acting strangely.

During the interview, one of the police officers, a man with short blond hair and beautiful hands, when I said this, about seeing the woman by the bins once at night, though I didn't say much of what I'd seen her doing, this I didn't think was really possible to say, reached into his bag and pulled out a picture of Nell and showed it to me.

Was it her? he asked me, jabbing the picture and I said no, it had been someone else. Have you seen her? he asked. Recently? Since the fire? She has two children, he said.

I said no, that I hadn't seen her at all, that I hadn't been near the apartment, that I'd only been out of the hospital for a few days, that we had been staying in a hotel by the lake. That we were leaving soon, in fact. Was that all right? I asked. Was I allowed to leave?

I was speaking too quickly, getting nervous. I was remembering the candles, the cups in the cupboards that were always filled with ash, and I was also quickly pushing all of those things away, pushing them far from me. I could feel sweat collecting on my upper lip and I wiped it with my un-bandaged hand. Of course it was all right, for me to leave. I was only there at the station for questioning, only there to help. I was the victim in all this, no one more than me, a young mother with babies to tend to. Soon, I was released back to my family, to my children, to M.

When I walked out of the station, M was waiting for me behind the steering wheel of our new car, the children were buckled up in their new Swiss-made car seats. I slid onto the soft leather seat on the passenger side and closed the door. M leaned across the sleek console, the GPS system, the touch-sensitive interfaces, and kissed me, and I buckled my seatbelt and M signalled and we turned out onto the road. I think you'll really like it, he said. What? I said. Our new place, he said.

Our new place, I said after him, repeating. Our new place, I said again, to myself, testing the words. It would be perfect. It would be a house with high ceilings and a view out over the lake and in the summer the days would balloon up inside with happy hot afternoons and in winter the snow would cover the tops of the mountains and we would marvel at the quiet of it, the way it covered everything up, the way that we were there, tucked away inside behind the windows, to see it. We could stand behind those windows looking out for years I thought, loving each other just like we did right now. Love could do that I thought, my love could, it could keep everyone young and happy and always together. I reached into the back seat and scrunched up E's toes, ran my fingers through B's hair. I am the only one for you, I thought. For all of you. The only one. What I'm trying to tell you is that that's what I was thinking when I went there, when M drove us to our new home. I was thinking of love.

We stopped at a buvette for lunch, one of those little places by the lake where the boats are all arranged in front, tied to the dock like swans with ropes around their necks. We ordered tall glasses of fresh orange juice with ginger and E went to go play in the grass, though really she just twisted the leaves off some bushes and whispered to her giraffe. Really mostly she just looked at me. I tried to smile in the right way but it was so unclear what she had seen in the fire that I was unsure how to act around her. I waved and M waved too.

We have to give her time, M said and I said yes, that was it. The juice was fresh and bright and every bit as good as it should have been. We ate egg and cucumber sandwiches that were made by the smiling bearded man who worked behind the counter. The sun felt like a gift on our shoulders. B tried a bit of egg, just a tiny smush. He smiled when it touched his lips. It was the first time that he'd had it, egg, and I thought that yes, of course, this is happiness, day after day of smushed eggs. Mornings and afternoons with all of us inside it. Juice and sandwiches. I want you to see that I wanted them all so badly, all those perfect days.

I left B with M and walked back to the counter and ordered espressos, two doubles. When they came to our table they were perfect. I smiled and M did too and our eyes got tangled up together and I saw ourselves when we used to drink stale diner coffee with so much sugar in it that it stung our tongues. How once we drove all night to get to one particular beach by sunrise. How we got to the beach just in time but fell asleep, nestling in the dirt beside the parking lot, holding hands. How we missed it all, and, of course, didn't miss a thing. I'm telling you this because I want you to see me there, sleeping by the car as the sun comes up. I want you to see me cooking salmon that was pink inside like kisses. I want you to understand that. I'm asking you to.

We said thank you to the man and drank the espressos which were excellent and exactly what we needed. We could have been anywhere, there beside a lake, coffee cups empty but still warm in our hands. M reached over the table and took my hand and yes, afternoons could happen this way. I could see it. For another hundred years. Dark coffee, white boats, blue lake. The sun would shine on our shoulders if we let it, it really would. If I believed this enough it would be true.

The new house will be perfect, M said. You will love it. You can see the boats on the lake from our bedroom.

But I'm trying to say that I felt it then, a hesitation. I want you to understand that I reached out to M. That I put my hand on his shoulder. That I rested my hand there long enough for me to have leant over and whispered into his ear, Let's not go, let's not.

And I almost did, say it I mean. M, Let's not.

See? I almost stopped it, everything.

When I looked up, I saw Nell sitting also at a table next to mine and she was holding her baby and drinking juice and I saw that her arms had burns all over them and I looked down and saw that I was also covered. That all the tables were filled with injured mothers drinking juice and faintly smoking, faintly disappearing into the air. Once we had a party or, wait, let me tell you once about a fire, please don't go and leave me with all these words sitting in my mouth. They're burning my lips.

Acknowledgements

Huge thanks and much gratitude to my amazing agent Jon Curzon, who rescued this book from the recycling bin. Thanks also to the rest of the team at Artellus for all their support and care.

Thanks to Sophie Jonathan for insightful editing and expert guidance, and for showing me how to turn a manuscript into a book. Thanks to everyone at Picador, I'm unbelievably lucky to be published by you.

Thank you to my family. Thanks to my parents, Mary Neerhout and Lane Borg, and thanks to my sister, Emma. Thanks to Kathy and Donna and Laura Jane. Thanks to Margaret and thanks to Jane.

Thanks to Dashiell, and Dexter, and Daley, my funny, my wise, my brilliant people.

Thank you also to my friends.

Thank you also, Alan, for everything.